My Dead World 4

JACQUELINE DRUGA

My Dead World 4 by Jacqueline Druga

Copyright © 2021 Jacqueline Druga

Published by Vulpine Press in the United Kingdom in 2021

ISBN 978-1-83919-170-1

www.vulpine-press.com

ONE

WHERE OR WHERE

Nila
July 14

His eyes were completely white and milky, like he suffered from triple layered cataracts, if that was even a thing. For a split second I thought of my Aunt Alice when her cataract surgery went bad.

She was blind for a while.

Which led me to wonder if the infected man could even see me? He stared at me as if he could, focusing, mouth moving in a vain attempt to bite me. A fence separated us, and I moved closer to it.

The eye thing was new. I was curious.

It was the third deader to come to our property in two days. The first with that new look. His skin hadn't decomposed too much, which told me he was fresh, only a few days perhaps. There were no bite marks on him I could see.

He'd turned. Got sick and turned. He was a survivor at one point. I could tell by his clothes and the fact he carried a hunting knife strapped to his right hip and a gun in a holster on his left.

I wondered if it was loaded.

His neck had the telltale traces of the virus—deep, dark veins that looked like a spiderweb traced to his chin.

1

The virus that brought the world to its knees had mutated, at least that was what we had learned when we stayed at Colony One.

The Colonies were government and military towns, with all the bells and whistles, gated up and guarded.

Those who lived inside were not only safe from the dead, but from what the world had become.

Safe until the walls fell, like they did in Colony One.

When that happened it seemed as if the entire network folded.

Of course, it just seemed that way. I wouldn't know. I was back home, on my land, in my father's cabin.

I thought about them a lot. The research they were doing to cure the virus and their desire to eradicate it by any means necessary, including killing the infected before they ever showed a symptom. On our road trip we saw evidence of that. Entire towns had been executed.

They were survivors.

Survivors that got sick.

But none of it mattered.

I was home.

My own world.

It just wasn't the same.

Not since it crumbled. Loss seemed to be a never-ending avalanche, picking up steam, gathering up those I loved and taking them away.

My daughter Addy, my husband, father, brother, and stepmother.

Friends.

I was eternally grateful my daughter Katie not only lived, but we also discovered she was completely immune to everything. Bites, the virus, any way she could get infected, she was shielded by her own masterful DNA. She was a potential cure, probably still could be. But in the mass confusion in the fall of Colony One, we didn't just slip away, we disappeared off radar.

With good reason.

I was grateful beyond measure for still having Katie, and I had to learn to grasp that, remember it, but I was having a hard time focusing on what I had, because I was reeling in what I had lost.

We went almost an entire year without losing anyone. In fact, we saw less and less of the dead.

It was over, I believed that. Life would start again, maybe some semblance of normalcy.

I was wrong; my belief couldn't have been further from the truth.

Heartache had been on a commercial break and it came back with a bang when I lost Lev.

Lev.

I had known him my entire life, from childhood, and it took for the world to drop to its knees to realize what kind of man, what kind of friend, he was. Lev was honest and let me know how things were. He didn't mince words or walk on eggshells with me. When I was wrong, he told me. When I acted badly or selfishly, he let me know. I could count on Lev for anything. And when I finally realized he was truly part of my soul, he was ripped from me.

My bravery in handling his death was a façade as weak as the walls that surrounded Colony One.

An illusion to benefit others when I knew how dark I felt inside. The endless nights of screaming into my pillow, sobbing myself to sleep, a pain in my chest that was as phys-ically real as it was emotionally.

It was like I was full of these emotions I needed to release, but I just didn't know how or if I even could.

Lev was the final death, the straw that broke the camel's back for me.

He was a symbolization, a cumulation of sorrow for every single person I loved deeply and who was gone.

Only three weeks had passed since he died, head on my lap on the porch of our cabin. He had caught the new strain of the virus, somewhere, somehow. We didn't know because there was still a lot to learn about it.

He decided to self-medicate and pass rather than chance dying and turning.

A noble way to go, but Lev deserved better. Like a hero's death. When he left, that pedestal I always placed him on got a lot higher.

It didn't feel like he was gone.

I could still smell him, feel him, and hear him as if he were still alive.

That's because I needed him to be alive.

The world was hard enough with him here; I didn't know how I was going to survive in it without him.

"Nila, are you going to take that out or stare at it the whole time?" It was strange, I could hear his voice. I closed my eyes, absorbing the sound. I swore I heard him.

His soft, yet sometimes condescending voice. It wasn't re-ally the way Lev was. He just sounded that way because he didn't use contractions much, and he still had a dusting of his Serbian accent which crept up once in a while.

"Do you need me to do it?"

My heart beat faster.

"Nila?"

Swept up in that weird moment, thinking of Lev and hearing his voice, I responded without thinking, "No, Lev, I got it."

"Fleck."

I briefly cringed when I realized it was Fleck who was talking to me. How did I not know or even hear the dog barking? A dreamlike veil was lifted, bringing me back to reality. "I know. I just…"

"It's okay. You need me to take him out?" Fleck asked.

I looked over at Fleck, he was poised and ready with an ice pick. "Nah." I reached out and took the pick. "I got it."

My new cataract friend gripped the fence, the skin on his fingers splitting as he held tight. He was calm, almost lacking motivation to get me.

I walked as close as I could to the fence, raised the pick and jammed it into his left eye. It didn't really do much until Fleck leaned in and smacked his palm against the end of the wooden handle, jamming it in all the way.

Then he went down.

"What was up with his eyes?" Fleck asked.

"I don't know. It's new." I withdrew the pick and handed it back to Fleck.

He pulled an old bandana from his back pocket and wiped it clean. "We should move him," Fleck said. "Far enough away that we don't catch his smell when the wind blows."

"It smells every time the wind blows, doesn't matter where we put them," I replied. "It just permeates the air."

"You're nuts. It's like skunk, you think you smell it even after it's gone."

"What the hell kind of comparison is that?" I asked.

"It's a good one. You wanna help me move him?"

"As long as we don't have to talk," I told him. "And I call dibs on his gun."

I walked past Fleck down the property line to the gate. As he trailed behind me, I heard him complaining that I always took the guns. I didn't understand what the big deal was. We all shared, and guns were useless to us unless we got overrun. In a quiet, dead world, up on that mountain, sound traveled for miles.

As we learned a long time before, a single weapon fired was like ringing the dinner bell. They found us with little problem as it was so we didn't need to make it any easier for the dead or whoever else happened to be out there lurking.

TWO

TUNE OUT

"What's wrong with her hand?" I asked the second I stepped back into the cabin.

Ben sat at the kitchen table with my daughter Katie. His glasses rested slightly downward on his nose as he examined Katie's hand like a palm reader.

"She got a splinter. A doozy of a splinter if I may say," Ben replied.

"How did she do that?"

"How does any child get the strange injuries they do," he spoke as he worked. "By doing something they aren't supposed to do."

"What did she do?"

"What does it matter?" Ben glanced up briefly, then back down to her hand. "Almost there."

Katie giggled. "There was a piece of wood sticking out of the cabinet under the sink," she said. "I pulled it out and thought it was smooth. When I rubbed it, it wasn't."

"Next time you'll learn," I said. I could smell something cooking in the kitchen. There was a kettle on the wood burning stove. A substance was brewing causing steam to rise and whip out a pleasant aroma. A welcoming smell after moving cataract man. The smell of food caused me to realize I was hungry.

I wondered who was cooking.

It was probably Meg making dinner, though I didn't see her. She was a newcomer to our group—she had only joined us a few weeks earlier.

A survivor from Colony One.

The cabin seemed so empty and quiet. It wasn't though. Ben and Katie were seated at the big, old wood kitchen table. Even Fleck barely took up any room. There were three other children with us, a baby, Sawyer, and Meg's daughter, Maura. Bella probably had the baby in the back bedroom and the others were likely to be outside.

There'd been a time, just over a year earlier, when there were so many people on the property.

Not only my father and stepmother and children, but Lev, his father, and other people from Big Bear campsite.

We hunkered down there, waiting it out.

Slowly, one by one, they all died.

Ben's son was with us back then as well. Cade.

That was how we'd met Ben. He came looking for his son. Following a message Cade wrote on a survivor wall when he went out looking for his father.

Cade never made it.

We were lucky to have Ben. He wasn't just some youthful grandfatherly type picking out a splinter. He was a surgeon. Albeit a plastic surgeon, but a doctor nonetheless. I heard he was an orthopedic surgeon or something before that. I never asked why he switched. He was a good, skilled doctor.

"There. Out," Ben announced, then lifted the tweezers. "Look at this. It's pretty big."

"I'm bleeding," Katie said.

"I see that." Ben winked. "We'll take care of it." He dabbed it with gauze, then slowly shifted his eyes to me. "We need antibiotics."

"We don't have any?"

"Unfortunately," Ben replied. "The last time we were here, before we left, Lev wiped us out. You went and got more but…he used most of them. On our trip back here we weren't packing a lot of medical supplies."

"She needs them?" I asked. "Not that I'm questioning your judgement. But does she need them now?"

"I have enough for today, but I'll have to go tomorrow."

"We'll go," Fleck called from the living room. "We need a supply run anyhow. We planted late, and we don't even know if they'll take."

"Then we go tomorrow," I said. "Ben, you just tell us what we need."

"Don't I always?"

I smiled. "Yes, you do." I was just grateful that for the time being the world was our own shopping mall. We had every big store imaginable within a fifteen-mile radius. There was enough out there remaining on the shelves that could last us a while.

There were more dead than living now and they didn't need canned peaches.

I watched as Ben bandaged my daughter's hand. It was hot in the cabin, even with the windows open. We had a solar generator we used to power the fridge and, for an hour or so a day, the back room with the tiny air conditioner.

At least at night the temperature dropped. Plus, we couldn't run the air, the noise was too much. We couldn't hear if anything approached.

9

As I ran my hand over my head to clear the sweat, I heard the sound of it.

Crackling and static.

The radio.

"Who is this again?" a male voice called out. "Can you repeat?"

My heart dropped to my stomach and I looked left to right, trying to determine where it had come from.

As soon as I remembered it was in the back room where we had stored the radio, I raced back there.

I burst open the door scaring Meg.

The young mom sat on my stepmother's sewing chair, staring at the radio while holding the microphone in her hand.

"What are you doing?" I asked with edge.

"It works," she said with a smile, so proud of herself. "I saw it. I did this for a living. Fixing things, you know. So I played around with it and it worked. I didn't think it would. I kept calling out and...listen." She lifted the received and pressed in the button. "This is Meg, are you—"

"What the hell is the matter with you?" Without a drop of hesitation, I pulled the microphone from her hand.

Meg seemed shocked, hurt, looking at me so confused. "What...why...?"

"There's a reason this radio was off. We don't call out. Ever." I shut the radio down with a hard smack with my hand. "Because we can't take a chance on who will respond."

THREE

AT THE END

Colonist, Sean Marshall
July 15, Burlington, VT

The tiny hand poked out of the rubble. It was the last straw. The dainty fingers with chipped pink nail polish wiggled and grabbed the air. The reasonable man in me knew the child was not alive. Not in the conventional sense, but a part of me feared she had been trapped in the rubble for three weeks, suffering and alone.

Knowing not much covered the child in the way of debris, I lifted the wood planks and bricks, until I exposed her face and upper torso.

Immediately, the little girl tried to lift up. Her arms swung wildly at me as she snarled and snapped her jaw.

"I can't." My throat was thick and the words barely came out. I coughed to clear my throat and raised my voice a little louder to be heard by my team. "Guys, I...I can't. I just can't."

It was at that moment I knew I was done.

I would finish my work there at the former site of Colony One. The people that had lived there were my family and friends. For them, and out of respect, I had to finish. We

11

were nearly done, as was my short tenure as a Captain for the Colonist division.

"Cap." One of my crew approached me. "You alright?"

"No, actually I'm not. I don't know how you guys keep doing it."

"Self-medication," he said. "Don't worry. We got this." He placed a hand on my shoulder and I turned after nodding a thank you.

No sooner did I turn, I heard the single gunshot. It went right through me.

Was that what it took to perform such a hard task? Self-medicate? Be numb to it all?

I didn't want to be numb to it all—feeling it was what kept me human.

It was a child, one probably no older than five or six. I knew the virus wasn't kind to the world, no matter who you were or how old, but we at The Colony were supposed to protect those who came into our fold.

Somehow we'd failed.

I'd failed as a leader.

Who was I kidding? I wasn't a leader. I wasn't even in the military. I had been a police officer in a small town. I was the cop known for giving out ridiculous amounts of traffic citations.

When the virus hit my town, I couldn't stay. I moved on. We tried everything we could to hold our ground, but it had been useless. Some remained, I left.

I wore my father's heavy green canvas jacket to protect my arms and thick blue jeans and boots so one of the crawlers didn't grab hold and bite.

They don't rip through jeans, their teeth aren't sharp enough. It wasn't a foolproof defense, though.

I was happy on my own. Walking place to place, everything I needed on my back. The world was full of supplies. There was no need to starve, not this early in the apocalypse.

It was never my intention to join up with a group.

But I happened upon a group of colony soldiers in trouble, so I lent a hand and the rest was history.

I did like what The Colony was doing. It was bringing back life. A person can survive, but living was vital. Living wasn't running every day of your life.

There were entire families who'd survived and were looking for a cure or antidote. We were working on the cure here day and night.

They were close.

And just like with Colony One, the chance for that cure slipped through their fingers.

More than I was willing to admit, I played a role in that.

I helped the key to their cure escape Colony One when it was overrun by infection and the dead.

It wasn't my intention to let the potential cure slip from our grasp. A cure which lies in the blood of a five-year-old. I only wanted to make sure she lived. I would never have thought, with her mother knowing how vital she was to the human existence, she would leave the evacuation center.

Where they went, if they'd survived, I didn't know.

There were rumors when the wall went down they had arrived in Cobb Corner. But in the short time I'd gotten to know the mother, Nila, it would have been closer and easier for her to go home to Pennsylvania. Back to a place she said was safe, rather than pass it and go all the way south.

We had successfully evacuated a little over four thousand out of the eight thousand in Colony One. An impressive feat in such a short period of time.

Things were hectic.

We were trying to keep those who were in early stages of infection from leaving, but also battling the dead and those who had recently turned.

We had to seal the area off.

That meant detonating the preset explosives.

Since it had happened twenty-five days earlier, my team and I had been uncovering and accounting for the lost. Living out of a campsite where the old school used to be.

As far as numbers went, we were close enough to stop.

Not to mention ready to stop.

We were near the point of calling it a day. Light was burning and it was only a matter of an hour or so before it got dark. I had a feeling, with so very few unaccounted for, we were going to be pulled.

Wrap it up and move on.

That feeling was confirmed when I heard the helicopter approaching.

I looked to the sky to see which direction it was coming from, and I watched it appear. From a black speck to a full-blown chopper. It flew in and lowered not far from where I stood.

The wind from the blades whipped and stung against my skin.

The chopper blades slowed down and then came to a stop. I didn't know who exactly it was, but it was someone important, because they could have radioed before coming here. They didn't.

The side door to the chopper opened. Deacon McCaffery, a self-proclaimed general of The Colony council, stepped off, along with Almada Hillgrove, a research doctor. I supposed since the death of Clare, Almada was now in charge.

She waved like I was an old lost friend as she made her way over.

"Captain," she said, then extended her hand. "I hear congratulation are in order. Everything ran smoothly."

"What percentage is left?" McCaffrey asked.

"We estimate less than ten percent of the population unaccounted for," I replied.

McCaffrey nodded. "They could have made it out."

"You run a tight ship here," said Almada.

McCaffrey sounded as if he scoffed. "Not so tight they don't follow our regulations." He rubbed his own chin, which I took as a reference to my own beard that had grown in the last month.

"Yeah, well." I rubbed my beard. "The dead don't care."

"Eh, I'm joshing you." McCaffrey winked.

Joshing? I thought. Who uses the word joshing anymore?

"Is that why you came?" I asked. "To check up on things?"

"Actually, we have two reasons," Almada said. "The first: we're excited because we confirmed where we are building the replacement Colony. It won't be as big as the others, but it's a perfect area. It will be research mainly."

"How did you find it?" I questioned.

"Just information given to us by those who were in Colony One. A lot of people suggested areas that were conducive to the project. We've been checking them out and finally settled on one."

"That's good." I nodded.

McCaffrey spoke, "We think we're finished here. And we'd like you and your team to be boots on the ground at the site first. Help clear it of any dead that remain and protect the building crews."

"I'm sure my crew will be happy," I replied. "And the other thing?"

"I'm sorry, what?" McCaffrey asked.

"The other thing," I repeated. "You said there were two reasons."

"That's right. Doctor?" He looked at Almada.

"Captain, I mean Sean, you spent more time than anyone with Nila Carter when they were in Colony One. You brought her on your team."

"I guess."

"In fact," Almada continued, "it was you who said you didn't think that was her and her group that went to Cobb Corner. Even though our soldiers said it was."

"It wasn't, Cobb Corner confirmed it," I said.

"You were right. That is why we are coming to you now. For your help. We need the little girl. We have not found another like her."

"That's because Canada was shooting anyone bitten, people are a little, for lack of a better word, gun shy," I replied. "I don't know what you want me to do. We don't know if they're alive."

"We think they might be. Can we go somewhere quiet?"

It was a strange request, but one I agreed to and I led her and McCaffrey to my tent.

"What's going on?" I asked once inside.

"Do you know where Nila is from?" Almada asked. "Her intake says southern Pennsylvania."

"I guess, she mentioned a little of her life when we were out. Not much. She worked at Arby's, that was about how personal we got."

"So she didn't mention any other place in Pennsylvania she lived or liked to go to."

"Um…" I shook my head. "Not detailed. Not really. Where is this coming from? I don't know her as well as you think. We hung out for like two weeks before the fall of Colony One."

"Two weeks in the apocalypse," McCaffrey said, "is like two years in the old world."

"Uh, yeah, not sure where that saying came from," I said. "Again, what's going on?"

"We've been scanning radio transmissions," Almada said. "Trying to find them, like we did last time. We picked this up yesterday." She nodded at McCaffrey.

He pulled a small device from his pocket that looked like a recorder, and he pressed play.

A woman's voice came over the tiny speaker.

"Anyone out there. Hello? Can anyone hear me? Hello?"

McCaffrey shut off the player. "She continued on like that until we responded."

"That's not her, I can tell you that," I said. "That woman has a distinct Vermont dialect. That's not Nila."

"We know," Almada replied. "That's not what we want you to hear."

McCaffrey pressed play again.

"We read you," a male voice said. "Identify yourself."

"My name is Meg Erickson, I'm with a group of survivors in Pennsylvania. Right now, we're fine. We're trying to locate other survivors."

Again, the player stopped.

"Meg Erickson and her daughter were in Colony One," Almada said. "I spoke to Meg many times, that's her voice. She disappeared about the same time as Nila."

"So you think Nila's with her?" I asked.

"You tell me. I haven't spoken to Nila. Listen and tell me what you think?"

With another nod, McCaffrey pressed play.

"This is Meg, are you—"

"What the hell is the matter with you?"

"That voice, the second female voice," Almada said. "What do you think?"

McCaffrey played it again.

"What the hell is the matter with you?"

I requested he play it once more and he did, then I shook my head. "Nah. It's not her."

"You don't think?" Almada asked. "Maybe if you listen to it one more time."

"It's not going to make a difference. I can listen to it a hundred times, and heck, maybe even convince myself it is her. But it's not. You're reaching."

McCaffery chuckled in ridicule. "It's not reaching. Meg Erickson disappeared after evacuation at the same time. That is Meg Erickson."

"What makes you so sure it's not Nila?" Almada asked.

"You said I spent more time with her than anyone else. I did. I know that's not her voice. And two, you said Pennsylvania, right?"

Almada nodded. "That's what Meg said."

"Think about it. Nila is smart. If Nila, Lev, and the gang left the evacuation center, they ran from us. They don't want to be found. She knows what she put on that intake. The last place she is going to go is to a place she knows you'll look. Listen again, Dr. Hillgrove. That second voice is deeper and raspy."

"But Nila has…"

I shook my head to stop her. "She did not have a deeper voice."

"Maybe she's just tired," McCaffrey suggested.

"It's not her. I'm sorry. It's not. Even if it was, I don't know where she would be. Pennsylvania is a big state."

Almada exhaled slowly and loud. "I guess not. It was worth a shot. We need to find her."

"I know," I said. "I'm sorry."

"We'll let you be," Almada said. "We're going to camp here tonight and help close up tomorrow."

"Thank you," I replied.

McCaffrey stepped to me. "We plan to leave in the late afternoon. Give you a chance to…" He rubbed his own chin. "Before you and your team go."

"Yes, sir," I replied.

They walked from my tent, leaving me alone.

Our work was done at Colony One. It was now official. We were moving out the next day.

Unlike everyone else, I wasn't shaving, nor was I heading to the new Colony site.

I was going off alone and my direction was elsewhere.

FOUR

ONLY HUMAN

Nila
July 15

It was beautiful and I recognized it right away. I couldn't help myself when I saw it. I stood a good distance from it, arms folded.

Fleck and I had gone to Butler to get more antibiotics and medical supplies for Ben. It wasn't the first time I had been down that way off the mountain, or on hospital grounds, but it was the first time I had seen it.

Did it just arrive?

Somehow I would have thought I would have noticed the large RV in pristine condition. It was parked at the end of the congested traffic that surrounded the hospital property.

"Nila," Fleck called my name. "That is not antibiotics."

"No, it's not. This wasn't here before."

"Yeah, it was."

"No, it wasn't."

"Nila, it was here before we even went to Florida. I recognize that blood smear on the side window."

"This is amazing. Someone stole this you know. Because it belongs to Big Bear. See the number on the door. BB-8. This was RV eight that they rented out."

"Big Bear, the campsite Lev and his father owned?"

"Yep, the very one." I folded my arms. "I think this was one of the ones taken when everyone panicked and left the camp. Lev was so pissed."

"I bet. And look, it was never far. Whoever took it died. All that blood, you know," Fleck said. "Maybe it's karma."

"Oh, that's not nice."

"Yeah, and this is coming from a woman who poisoned the well."

I faced him, my jaw dropping slightly. "I can't believe you brought that up."

"That's not something you easily forget. Now let's go, the longer we stand here, the more chance we have of the deaders coming out."

I looked again at the RV. Lev and his father were so proud to have them and rent them out. They were beautiful and slept six, or maybe it was eight.

"Nila, come on."

"I think we should take it."

"What? Why would we do that?"

"Because we need it," I replied. "Right after the outbreak, we had people stay on my father's land. Edi, her husband. Fleck, you saw we had two trailers there before."

"Which we moved; they were fucked up."

"They were. But this, I bet we can clean this up. We need to clear the cabin. Right now, there's me, Katie, you, Ben, Bella…"

"Yeah, I get it. There's nine people."

"All in the cabin. If we give people space, they will be happier."

Again, Fleck laughed. "You just want people out of your house."

"That too."

"The idea is good. I'd like to not sleep on a chair. Why don't we see if we can find one or two not damaged?"

"I really want this one," I said.

"Why this one?"

"Because it belonged to Lev and his father."

"That's a pretty insane reason to keep it. You want to keep a fucked-up RV for sentimental reasons, when I know for a fact, there's an RV 'park and storage' right outside of Cranberry. Filled with RVs that people didn't die in."

"We don't know anyone died in there," I said.

"The big blood smear on the window is a good indication."

"But the blinds are down," I defended. "That happened after the blood. Deaders don't do that."

"You're impossible when you get something in your mind. I mean, what would Lev say?"

"Is that on the same line of what would Jesus do?"

"Really?" Fleck shook his head.

"Okay, Lev would…" I paused, and in an instant, I could hear his voice.

"Nila, as nice as it is that you want to do this, there are better options. Go to the Cranberry RV Park and Storage."

"He would tell me to check it out first," I said.

"Okay, fine, we'll check it out. When you see it's bad, can we move on?"

"Can we get an RV?"

"Today? You want to go today?"

"It's early," I said. "Really we need one. Or two."

"It's a lot more complicated than just getting in the RV and going. The battery will be dead after all this time. No jumping, we'd have to go get one…and…" He stared at me. "Fine. But we get the antibiotics first, take them back and go get the big truck in case we need to jump a battery."

"Thank you."

"Now this." Fleck walked to the door of the RV and banged his hand once.

"I don't hear anything," I said, standing next to him. "Usually they clamor."

"Usually."

I leaned toward the door. "I'm still not hearing anything."

"You smell anything?" Fleck asked. "Because I am gonna bet the stench…what was the word you used, permeates, yeah that was it. I bet it permeates the place."

"It doesn't really fit in this instance," I rebutted. "Let's do this." I reached for the crowbar dragging down my belt loop.

"You first." He latched his fingers on the small metal door handle, stepping to the side for me as he pulled.

The door swung open and out lunged a deader. Full force with a snarling leap.

The deader wasn't small, he was bigger and after his hands grabbed for me, the weight of him knocked me right over and on to the ground. I felt the small of my back connect with the concrete, then my head cracked against it as well. I didn't register the pain, I was too busy trying to push him off, or at least keep his mouth away. He snarled and snapped, and not only was it the most horrendous smell, right there, blasting my face, my hands just sunk into his slimy flesh. It felt like I was trapped beneath him forever, that I struggled for the longest time, but that probably wasn't the case.

23

Fleck took him out, I saw the icepick go into his head and the deader dropped down to me.

I tried to move him, but my hands just sunk further. I could feel the mush his organs had become. Fleck tried to kick him from me, but his foot did the same thing as my hands. Just went right into him. Finally, Fleck lifted him off and grunted with disgust.

"What the hell?" Fleck shook his hands, the stringy, clear substance just kind of whipped around.

It reminded me of the rubber cement glue I used in school, and it covered the deader in a thick coat.

Fleck kept trying to flick it off, and he groaned with his futile attempts.

Was he really complaining? I was still on the ground, the stuff was all over me, not to mention up to my forearms I was covered with insides.

It was gross and worse than the deader I had put in the pool house up at Big Bear early in the outbreak.

I rolled to my side and felt the slight pain in my hip, but it was nothing compared to the instant throbbing headache I experienced.

Between the pain in my head and the stench, the moment I stood, I wobbled to get my balance, took a few steps away and vomited.

"What the fuck was all over it?" Fleck asked.

"I really can't…" I heaved again, my stomach twisting and turning. "Can't answer you right now. Oh, God, that smelled so bad." Just when I thought I was under control, I saw the stuff on my arms and fought to not throw up again.

It wasn't like me to get sick from it, maybe I was still in some sort of sensitive state.

"Ug!" I heard Fleck grunt again. "I'll get the jug from the car."

I nodded, still half bent over.

"I know what it was," Fleck said. "Hot car syndrome."

"What?" I asked, confused, and stood upright. I turned and instinctively began bringing my arm to my mouth to wipe, but thankfully caught myself before I smeared dead guts all over. I opted for my shoulder and top of my arm to clear my chin.

"Hot car syndrome." Using that damn dirty bandana, Fleck wiped off one of his hands and opened the station wagon door, reached in, and grabbed the gallon water jug. He placed it on the ground, careful not to touch the jug at all with his other hand. "When someone gets locked in a hot car with no air, they kind of melt from the inside out, and I bet that's what happened to him."

He washed off his hands.

"We're gonna need more than this. Soap maybe," he said

"New clothes," I said.

He carried the jug to me. "I have never seen that on them and we've seen a lot. Hold out your arms."

"There's not enough water in that jug to clean my arms."

He looked around. "Well, we're not far from the hospital. We can find something there to clean off with."

"Hopefully the barricade held so we don't run into any deaders. I whacked my head."

"You okay?" Fleck asked, rinsing off my arms and using the last of the water.

"Yeah." I shook my arms to dry them, then wiped them on the side of my pants.

"Sorry I said you first." Fleck bent down for my crowbar on the ground. "It was quiet. Probably because it was…dude, you're bleeding."

"What?" I asked, shocked.

"The back of your head."

I reached up and he stopped me.

"Don't touch your open wound," Fleck instructed. "Until we get cleaned up better."

"Open wound?"

"It's bleeding pretty bad."

"Head wounds always do," I said.

"Let me get something from the car to put against it."

"Just not your bandana."

I watched him head back to the car. I knew there'd be something in there. Lev got me in the habit of keeping supplies in the car in case we got stuck. He fussed around in the back, then shut the door with his hip before returning to me.

"Sanitizer." He held up the bottle, then placed a few squirts in my hands.

As I rubbed it in, he placed the small bottle in his back pocket and gave me a cloth.

"Put that on your head." He guided my hand to where I should place it. "You don't feel that?"

"My head hurts too bad." As soon as the cloth touched my scalp, I felt the stinging. "I feel it now. I think I have a concussion."

"Are you alright to do this?" he asked.

"I'll be fine. We need to get those supplies."

It really wasn't that far. The amount of cars hadn't changed since the last time we were there. It was about a quarter of a mile from where we had to leave the car to the entrance of the emergency room.

I was really fretting it until we started walking. I tried focusing on the pain in my hip to divert attention from the pain in my head. It moved to my eyes. Every time my heart beat, I felt a throb of intense pain.

It felt like ten miles, but I didn't want to let Fleck know I was feeling poorly with each step I took. Other than wanting to vomit again, I was extremely thirsty, and every time I thought about the fact that there wouldn't be drinkable water at the hospital, my thirst grew stronger.

I tried anything to take my attention off of how I felt, looking in cars, hoping to spot a bottle of water. It was impossible to see inside because a year's worth of dirt covered the windows.

When I could see inside, it just made me feel worse. The corpses in the cars were mummified, and the half-eaten ones exposed to the elements were almost pure skeletons, with the exception of the leathery skin that remained.

"It held," Fleck announced as we moved closer to the ER.

He was referencing the bench and garbage cans we'd placed in front the doors. It didn't really protect anything. The glass on the doors had been busted for a while, long before we even went there. The bench with the stacked garbage cans were more of a blockade and warning system. If they were moved or disturbed, someone or something had made it inside.

"At least none came in this way," he said.

When we arrived at the entrance, I had to stop.

Mid moving the bench slightly, enough to slip through, Fleck asked me again if I was alright. I told him I was, just really thirsty from throwing up.

"We can bust into that vending machine in the waiting room," he said.

"If it's still intact."

"If the barricade held inside, it will be. I thought it was odd you guys never raided it."

"There was never a need," I replied.

"You don't look well."

"I don't feel well."

"Give me the list." He held out his hand. "I'll grab the stuff."

I reached into my pocket and grabbed the list. "You sure?"

"Positive. Let's get inside out of the heat. But let me check first."

I nodded and Fleck went inside. I turned to keep an eye out for dead. I spotted one in the distance. Just one, weaving in and out of cars, looking at them, just like I had done. I squinted, because for a moment, I wondered if it was a deader.

"Clear," Fleck said. "Barricade held."

"Is that a deader or survivor?" I asked.

"You can't tell? That's a deader."

"I can't see that far right now."

"Man, wow, let's get you inside."

There was a small security check area as soon as we entered. Fleck grabbed the swivel chair, rolling it though into the reception area.

I shut the security door behind me, just in case the wandering deader found its way to us.

It was darker inside, but not impossible to see. Sunlight seeped through the windows of the waiting area.

"Sit." Fleck pushed the chair to me.

Immediately I did. I was feeling worse by the second, and the heat didn't help at all. Along with being sick to my stomach, I was dizzy, too. I didn't need to be Ben to know for sure I had a concussion. I'd had them before, I just didn't remember feeling as bad so fast.

Opening the vending machine caused a loud bang to ring out, and in turn alerted the dead that were in the hospital. I could hear the immediate sound of them pounding against the doors, rattling them.

I wasn't worried. I knew they wouldn't get through.

Fleck handed me a bottle of water and a soda, then went into the back. Immediately, I started drinking the water.

He would be safe. Nearly a year before, when Lev nearly died in Canada, Fleck and I went to the ER. It was after the initial trip Ben and I made. More supplies were needed for Ben to replenish his medical stock. We decided then and there, in case we ever had to come back, we'd make it as easy and safe as possible.

That was Fleck's idea more than mine.

So we made sure after we cleared the few deaders, and we secured that ER, the supply area, and pharmacy to keep them out.

It worked.

I was glad, I wasn't in the mood to battle and didn't feel up to it physically. It was like an anomaly to me, feeling so horrible. On top of the pain in my hip and head, my shoulder ached from holding the rag to my head.

I lowered it and brought it around to look. There was a lot of blood. The blood stain on the cloth blurred and then doubled. I felt like I needed to reach for glasses.

That was when it dawned on me, sure, I had been sick and injured in my life, but it was the first time since the outbreak that I was hurt. Everyone else had their share of injuries. Not me.

I felt weak and stupid at that moment. The pain increased in my head. I didn't think that was possible. I wanted to scream it hurt so badly. I wanted to holler out for Fleck to get me something for the pain, but in that instant, I couldn't even remember his name.

I didn't know what it was, it was one of those moments where it was on the tip of my tongue. In fact, I started to get confused. Why was I there? How did I get hurt? Why was I in pain? I closed my eyes trying to think.

Think, Nila, think.

"Nila," his voice called softly to me almost internally inside my head rather than outside my ears.

I opened them. My vision was even more blurry, everything looked dreamy.

I swore I saw Lev crouched down before me. I knew he wasn't real, that it was my mind reaching out for the one person who was always there when I needed him.

"I know it hurts," Lev said. "Remember when I hurt my head when we were twelve."

I nodded.

"Are you tired?"

"So tired. I'm going to go to sleep, Lev."

"Nila, don't go to sleep. Nila, open your eyes."

"I can't. I'm tired, Lev. I'm so tired."

I was. My head bobbed forward, feeling so heavy, it was hard to lift. The rag slipped from my hand, the pain, while still there, lessened as I drifted off.

"Nila, wake up. Stay with me. Don't go to sleep."

I could feel the vibration and the movement. My eyelids fluttered, opening slightly to the bright sun. I was in the car.

"Groan or something," Fleck said.

"I'm fine, Lev."

"Sure you are. Just try not to sleep. I don't know if that holds true or not about falling asleep. Nila, wake up."

Suddenly his voice became my own, back to that night after Lev was beaten within an inch of his life. Spending the night in the car, constantly calling his name to get a reaction from him. I wasn't that bad, was I? I didn't hit my head that hard.

Was I so consumed with worry over that deader I never knew how hard I hit the pavement?

Despite Fleck's best attempts to keep me awake, I fell asleep again, waking to Ben's voice.

"Let me get this straight," Ben said. "You pushed her from the hospital in a rolling office chair. How did you keep her in the chair?"

"Duct tape," Fleck replied.

"That was smart."

"What?" I heard my sluggish sounding voice as I tried to move. "My arms are tied."

"No, they aren't," Ben told me. "You're back at the cabin."

"I'm fine."

Fleck laughed. "When I came back from the supplies, she was having a conversation with Lev."

"How hard did she hit her head?" Ben asked. "I need to staple the gash. But the head splits easily."

"Honestly," Fleck replied, "I don't know. We were too busy with the deader that attacked her."

"Yeah, I can smell it on her," Ben said.

"I smell?" I asked.

"Yes, we'll get you cleaned up. But first, Nila, open your eyes all the way for me."

I did, and held them open as much as I could. A bright light flashed in my eyes and I squinted.

"Open them, Nila," Ben instructed.

It took all I had to keep them open with that light in my eyes.

"Okay, well, the pupils are not reacting very fast. More than likely it's a concussion," Ben said. "I don't see any fluid in her nose or ears, so that's a good sign."

"She threw up almost immediately," Fleck said.

"The thing smells and it was gross," I said. "I'm fine. Really. Just a little groggy. We have to go get the RV."

Ben looked at Fleck. "RV? Is that another illusion like Lev?"

"No, that's real," Fleck replied. "We were gonna head to Park and Storage and grab an RV for the property. More space for everyone."

"That's a good idea. However, she's not going anywhere yet. Her getting up from that fall and walking to the hospital did more harm than good. So she has to rest."

"Can I rest without my name being called every five minutes?" I asked.

"Yes," Ben told me. "After I fix that gash."

Without groaning or complaining, I gave him my agreement. I really wanted to go get that RV, but wasn't feeling up to it and doctor's orders were to rest.

I hated being down and out. But at least I was down and out on my own couch, on my property in the safety of my home. To me, there was no safer place to be.

FIVE

FREEDOM AFTER FIVE

Sean Marshall
July 16

I left before daylight. It wasn't the smartest thing to do. The dead were hard to see at night, and I had to rely on the scent. Although the night vision goggles did seem to help.

More than anything I wanted to take one of the jeeps or trucks, but I couldn't bring myself to do that to my crew. I took only the very few personal belongings I had, my weapon, ammo, a radio to monitor things, and two bottles of water. The rest I could find on the road.

The night before was normal, with the exception that Almada and McCaffrey were there. They had dinner with the crew, laughing and chatting. They talked up the new place for the colony, mentioning that they didn't see many dead on the ground.

The crew was amped up to go clear the town, as if taking out the dead was a fun thing to do.

It was disturbing to me. Always had been.

As cold and collective as I put on about clearing them outside the perimeter of Colony One, it bothered me.

The hard part was the beginning of the journey, right after leaving camp. I had to head south—I could walk and I would if I had to, but my best chance of getting a head start would be to get transportation.

I didn't know if The Colony would look for me or simply say 'screw him' and head off on their merry way. There weren't any AWOL regulations that I was aware of. Still, the way I knew they did things, creating rules as they went along, I wasn't taking any chances.

There were cars and some other vehicles at the evacuation center, whether they worked or not remained to be seen.

The evacuation center was the receiving center before Colony One fell. A former hotel transformed into the first stop for survivors and new residents. Safe and secure, those entering the colony often left their cars there.

The last time I was there, inside the building, was to get Nila her gun so she and I could go perimeter hunting. The keys to their vehicle, along with other keys, were in an envelope neatly stacked in a metal bin.

That was my goal. To get there and to that office.

But to do so I had to walk the three-mile stretch of road between Colony One and the center. An open road. Any and all buildings on both sides had been cleared and knocked down, so there was no coverage from the dead.

When we evacuated Colony One, that was the route the buses took. It had become so overrun with the dead, we had to firebomb the road.

We lost two of the buses.

That stretch of road scared me.

I walked it with the night vision, opting not to use my flashlight.

I hadn't been on that road at all since the fall. I was seeing it for the first time through the green glowing tiny holes of my goggles.

The smell of it hit me just before the sight of it. Rotting flesh that smelled as if it had been charcoaled. The road was scattered with debris, and there were deep divots that I imaged were from the explosives. Then I saw the bodies.

They were charred, some in pieces, and those still attached to a head moved. Their eyes glowed when I looked at them.

The dead were still moving.

I had to be careful.

My heart raced with each step I took. I realized how much bravery I lacked when I wasn't with others. It wasn't that way when the outbreak first began. I was happy to be alone, never too fearful. Now I was like a kid walking in the dark, shaking at every sound or movement.

A mile before the center, I saw an evacuation bus on its side. The windows were broken and bodies of the deaders covered it. They had attacked the bus before the road was bombed.

It was the long walk of death, and I was glad to see the evacuation center.

I arrived there just as the sun began to lighten the sky. About the time they would realize I was gone. Maybe not. Maybe they would think I was still sleeping or in the john. I glanced down to the radio clipped to my belt. The green light was lit, the battery was still strong. Even with low volume there was no sound, no chatter. That was a good sign. I'd hear it if they were looking for me and calling out.

I hoped it would take them a while to figure it out. I wanted miles between us. At that moment, the only distance between us was that stretch of road.

The gate was closed, latched, but not locked. I was able to open it and lock it behind me.

There was an eerie feel to the dark building. No sounds, no dead walking about.

Every person that had been there was long since had gone.

I walked around the hotel to the front lot. There were at least a dozen vehicles parked there.

Not taking a chance, I pulled out my pistol and went inside to seek out the office with the keys. I banged on the front desk counter, hoping to call out any dead that were there.

None came.

Making my way around the front desk, I went to the office in the back and used my flashlight. It was in disarray, no longer neatly organized as it had been. Someone had been in there, searching.

The envelopes with names, the ones once neatly lined up in a bin were on the floor. I shined my light on them, then crouched to the ground feeling each and every one until I found one that felt as if it had a set of keys.

Bingo.

Found three.

Looking at the dates, I took the one that was the newest.

That was my best chance for a working car.

I ripped open the envelope and let the keys fall into my palm. It had one of those key fob clickers on the chain. I prayed in my mind the car wasn't dead.

I hurried back outside.

In those few minutes the summer sky had lit up even more. I held my breath, raised the key fob, and pressed it.

Blip-blip.

Yes!

I was so excited I didn't see the car's flashing lights.

So I pressed it again.

The parking lights blinked on a small black car two rows away and I rushed over there.

Just as I unlocked the driver's door, my radio hissed, causing me to nearly jump out of my skin.

"Captain Marshall, you read? Cap?"

Hand on the car door, I glanced down to the radio.

"Cap, come in. Are you there? Do you read?"

"Yeah," I said to myself. "I read. But I'm not answering."

I opened the car door, tossing my few belongings inside, then I slid into the seat.

With a 'please, please, please' I placed the key in the ignition and turned it.

It started.

Filled with excitement, I closed the door and looked at the gas gauge.

A little less than half a tank. It wasn't a lot, but I would cross that bridge when I got there. For the time being, it was enough.

Hearing them call for me one more time, I shut off the radio, put the car in gear, and hurriedly drove off.

SIX

BIG BANG

Nila
July 18

I swore I'd had enough rest over a period of three days, that I wouldn't have to sleep for the longest time.

Hating to admit it, that bump to the head took me out of commission for the first twenty-four hours after it happened. I lacked energy to do very much, constantly micro napping.

My daughter Katie never left my side. Or at least it seemed that way.

She had this twisted habit of drawing events that happened with disturbing graphic accuracy on a child's level of artistic ability.

When Lev was injured, she drew him getting beat up. She drew Corbin being shot in the head. When Lev died, she drew him in heaven with my father, her father, and Addy.

For me, she did wonderful pictures of my head being huge and bloody, my eyes dark like the dead. Perhaps that was the way she saw me.

She kept me company constantly.

But she, like me and probably everyone else, was growing tired of the commune that the cabin had become. Katie wanted to play with Sawyer, but since Maura arrived and was

39

closer to his age, Katie was the third wheel. They didn't push her away on purpose, she was young.

Katie was ready to have her home back.

When I woke and washed my face, she carefully carried a cup of coffee up to me even though the liquid splashed about with every step she took.

Her way of warming me up.

"Mommy, is today the day you go get the houses on wheels for everyone?"

I thought about it for a second, tapped into how my body felt. "You know what? Yeah. We can get at least one today."

"Who is going to go in there?"

"I don't know. Fleck says he wants one."

"Fleck can get one like Edi had. Small."

"That's right." I sipped my coffee and thanked her. The taste of it told me Ben had brewed it. He always made it a bit strong.

"Are you feeling better?" she asked.

"Yes, yes, I am," I told her even though a part of me didn't feel a hundred percent.

I enjoyed a bit more of my coffee, it was still early and I figured I'd find Fleck to see if he was up to hitting the park and storage place for RVs.

Pack up the jumper cables, the charger, and head on out.

I stepped out of the bedroom into the living room. Ben was sitting there with Bella and Meg.

"Nila," Bella said brightly. "You look better."

"Thanks, I feel better," I replied. "Anyone seen Fleck?"

"He's outside," replied Bella.

"Hey," Ben called out. "You aren't thinking of making the RV run today, are you?"

"I was thinking about it."

"You think that's wise?"

"You're the doctor, you tell me."

"As long as you feel better," he said.

"I do."

"Then I suppose that would be fine. It's not like you're doing anything too strenuous."

"No. I'm gonna"—I pointed to the door—"see if Fleck is up for the run."

Meg asked, "Can you pick up some supplies?"

"Do we need stuff?"

"I mean no," she answered. "But we can use it. So just in case, maybe we should always be as fully stocked as we can."

"Then we'll stop."

"Nila," Ben called me again. "Only if you feel up to it."

Waving him off, I scoffed and said, "I'm fine." Then with my coffee in my hand, I opened the front door.

The second I stepped out there, I knew I wasn't exactly a hundred percent.

Maybe it was the fact that it was the first time in a long time I'd stopped moving and my body needed to just get motivated again.

I heard Katie's dog barking. That alarmed me—usually when he barked it was because something was wrong or a deader had made its way to the property.

But he was joyfully running about in circles, chasing something Fleck was tossing his way.

Fleck saw me and waved. "You feeling better?"

"Yeah," I replied. "I want to finish this and was thinking we could head out."

Fleck gave a thumbs-up. "As long as you feel better."

I was better. My head didn't hurt anymore, but my stomach was still off. No sooner did I lower to sit on that top step, my favorite place of the cabin, a wave of queasiness hit me.

"Oh, boy," I said softly, and brought my lips down to my coffee. As the warm brew crossed my lips, the porch screen door slammed and the patter of feet ran across the wooden planks of the porch.

"Here, Mommy." Katie handed me a cracker.

"Thanks, honey but…"

"Hey!" she shouted as she raced down the steps and across the yard. "Fleckenstien, don't! I am training him!"

I watched as she retrieved her beagle and with a quick double clap of her hand, she ran off to the side of the cabin with the dog following her.

Fleck, shaking his head, headed back to me. "That…is one really strange kid."

"Why?" I laughed. "Because she's training the dog?"

"No, because she called me Fleckenstien. That's my real last name. How did she know that?"

I didn't have an answer, because I didn't even know that was his last name. All I could do was mutter the word, "Strange," and look down to the cracker she had handed me.

I had to admit, a conversation with Fleck was interesting. In the past it just consisted of his snide comments about things, especially about my daughter. They weren't really in depth. I blamed myself because I gave all my conversation time to Lev.

Now, they were different. Granted he still went off about Katie. Nothing mean, but definitely comments from a man who didn't have children.

The whole trip to the RV place was about Katie knowing his name. Then he went off about the dog and he didn't stop.

It made me laugh. "Why do you care?"

"Because it's the family dog. She has to share."

"She does?"

"No, she doesn't. She yelled at me for teaching it fetch. I asked her about it, do you know what she said?"

"What?"

"She asked if I would teach a nine-year-old to go potty. She's five, Nila, what five-year-old talks like that?"

"Katie is around a lot of adults. That's why. What about this one?" I asked, stopping at a smaller RV. I banged on the door as a warning.

"Yeah, that's good. What is she training it?"

"Who knows. I like this one. It's small." I grabbed for the door and paused. "You stand in front this time."

He did. "Maybe I should train Katie to pick up the dog poop."

"You should."

"Maybe then she'll share her dog."

"Did you ask her?" I carefully opened the door, swinging it out so if anything jumped forth it would hit Fleck.

"I did. I said really nicely, can we share your dog?"

I got he wanted to talk about it, but I wanted to pick an RV so we could get it ready to move. First step was going inside to make sure it was fine. When it was clear nothing was in the small RV, I stepped inside. Fleck followed.

"What was her reply? Keep in mind, she's five."

"Why is her young age only an excuse when she says something I don't like?"

"Do you like anything she said?" I looked around. "Oh, this is really cute. We can put that new bossy woman Meg in here."

Fleck laughed. "She's not bossy. You just don't talk to anyone. No."

"Huh? No? You don't like this one? It's not like we're shopping. You can pick one you like for you."

"No, I mean, Katie said no. I told her I always had a dog growing up."

Fleck stayed in the kitchen and sitting portion of the RV and I walked to the back. There was a nice closet and a bathroom. Only one bedroom, but more than that wasn't needed.

"She told me…" Fleck spoke from the other room. "I was going to get my own dog soon. Now how the hell is that gonna happen?"

"We don't really need another dog, Fleck."

"Nila, this isn't like a family decision where there are too many pets in the house or who is gonna take care of it."

I walked from the back to join him. "How long to get this road ready?"

"We have to let it charge for about twenty minutes before we move it. We can go hit the Brite Pharmacy for some of that list."

"Good idea."

"Don't you like dogs?" Fleck asked.

"Not particularly."

"Cat person?"

"Hardly."

"What?" Fleck asked in shock. "What kind of person doesn't like animals?"

"I didn't say I didn't like animals, just not dogs and cats. Can we get this ready?"

"Yes. What animals do you like?"

"What does it matter?"

"Did you ever have a pet?"

"Fleck," I snapped his name. "Who cares about this right now? And yes, I had a pet. We had a pet pig at the cabin."

"See, better, more human. How long did you have him?"

"Until he was big enough for my dad to slaughter."

"Nila, that constitutes a farm animal. Not a pet."

"Oh…my…God, please stop. Grab your tools, let's get this ready and go to the pharmacy. Worry about your weird obsession with dogs another time."

"It's not a weird obsession. I love dogs. Just wish Katie was right and I'd find my own. But what are the chances?"

Woof.

My eyes widened.

His eyes widened.

Slowly at the same time we turned our heads to the sound.

Woof.

"I swear to God, your daughter is fucking weird." He barreled to the door.

"Stop," I called out just as he reached the door. "What if it's a setup or it's some zombie dog?"

"It's not a zombie dog. It would sound different." He hurriedly opened the door.

It could have been a lot of things, including bad people, he was just so unsuspecting because he wanted it to be a dog so badly.

When I heard him talking in that high voice, saying, "Who's the good boy? Who? That's right," I knew it was safe and I stepped out.

Sure enough, tough guy Fleck was like a little boy with his dog. The brown lab looked so grateful as well.

"Look at him, Nila. Oh man. Katie is gonna be so pissed that my dog is bigger."

"I don't think she'll care because you'll leave her dog alone."

"No tags." Fleck examined its neck. "I'm gonna call you Three Sixteen," he spoke happily.

"I didn't know you were particularly biblical or spiritual."

"What does that have to do with the name?"

"Um, John Three Sixteen is a famous bible quote."

"What is it?"

I shrugged. "I don't know. I just know that it is."

The dog had its paws on Fleck's shoulders as Fleck pet him. "Well the name has nothing to do with the bible. It's after a famous wrestler. And you like it," he upped his voice again. "Don't you boy."

"It's a girl," I said. "I don't see a penis."

"Why…are you looking and it doesn't matter." Fleck stood. "I wonder if she knows how to sniff the dead."

"The bigger question should be, where did she come from? She looks healthy, not malnourished. Someone has been taking good care of her. She's not mean. So her owner is around here."

"Are you saying we should look?"

"Yeah, I am. I mean if you lost your dog wouldn't you hope someone would try to get him to you."

"Aw, goddamn it." Fleck stomped. "Let's look."

"It can't be far," I said. "The dog didn't just wander on to this lot, there's no water or food source. Ask her."

"Where's your friend, girl? Huh?"

The dog barked.

"Where is he? Show me. Come on."

The dog moved in circles then took off running.

"I swear if I lose her, it's on you," Fleck said, following the bouncing lab.

I wasn't as blind as Fleck, and was much more cautious. The moment I turned the bend, I pulled out my pistol. The lot was huge and there were a ton of RVs and tractor trailers. It was like a scary maze. My anxiety level instantly increased, reminding me of the days when my husband, Paul, thought a good date night was going to one of those haunted houses. I hated them and hated when someone jumped out at me.

Fleck was a good twenty feet ahead of me, staying steadily behind the dog. Then the dog just stopped, causing Fleck to stop as well. This gave me a chance to catch up.

The dog didn't bark. Its hind legs moved back and she kept on nudging into Fleck as if pushing him.

"Something is there," I said, backing up slightly. "She's warning you."

"I don't hear anything." He looked to his right and to the RV. "Maybe one is in there."

Still, Three Sixteen kept using her body to move Fleck.

"Fleck, she's telling you to back up."

Fleck put his back against the RV, inching forward to peek around. That made the dog even more determined.

Something was there. I sensed it, and the lab was truly trying to move Fleck.

I couldn't smell anything, at least anything that smelled strong enough to be close.

The dog went wild, but with its body, not vocally.

"What?" Fleck asked her, then peeked again around the side of the RV. "What is it girl? I swear there might be something wrong with this dog. I don't see anything."

Then I saw it. The arms, there had to be six of them reaching out from under the RV.

"Fleck!" I called out. Immediately my mind flashed to that moment in the drug store with Cade when one of them, on the floor, bit him on the leg.

Even with my call of warning and the dog, they grabbed on to his leg.

I replaced my pistol and lifted my crowbar, racing forward.

When they grabbed for his leg, it took Fleck by surprise and he lost his balance, catching himself before he slammed to the ground.

He tried to kick his leg to free himself, and he reached for the ice pick.

"Fucking look at their eyes," he said. In the position he was in, it was nearly impossible for him to reach far enough to get an effective head blow.

Even the angle was difficult for me. His foot was partly under the RV, so getting the heads of the dead was tough. I could shoot, but that would be a bad angle as well.

Even the dog knew better than to bite them.

She started barking loudly.

One crawled out from under the RV. He was fast on his belly. The deader was missing his lower limbs and, like a snake on speed, he slithered his way up to Fleck.

That one I could get.

I brought down the crowbar hard, hooking it into the skull, deep enough to drop it.

"Pull your leg, Fleck," I shouted then reached for his leg.

"I'm trying. It's like the movie The People Under the fucking Stairs, they are pulling."

I grabbed hold of his legs, trying to free him as well, but they had him good.

"They're biting my boot. I can feel the pressure."

I had to think. It should have been an easy free, it should not have been a problem for him to get loose. But for some reason the five that remained weren't letting go unless they had another focus.

Telling Fleck to get ready I moved a few feet from him and got down on the ground on my stomach.

I banged the crowbar against the concrete then the side of the RV, calling out to them.

Sure enough their attention was caught and they scurried my way.

Unlike Fleck, I was ready for them and scooted back so they would have to emerge enough for us to get them.

The first one's head emerged, and Fleck got it. I was fearful of standing, because I didn't want them to retreat under there where they could surprise us at a later time.

I remained the bait, vulnerable on the ground as Fleck eliminated them one by one.

Three Sixteen finally calmed down and that told me, at least I hoped, there weren't any more around.

With Fleck's help, I stood and dusted myself off.

"You okay?" he asked.

"I'm fine. You?"

"The outside of my boot is fucked up."

"They didn't bite you, right?"

"No."

"Good." I bent down to Three Sixteen. "Thank you, girl. Good girl. When we get back I'll give you a treat."

"That's my dog you know."

"I know it's your dog," I said.

"We just do not have luck with RVs, do we?" Fleck asked.

He was right, we were two for two with deader attacks on the RVs. And if we didn't want to press our luck any further, I knew we had to prep the one I picked, get some supplies, and head back.

We did search.

We took one more walk around the lot and the area. Sure enough, the sadness moan that came from Three Sixteen told us we had found her owners.

A young couple, maybe in their thirties. They'd set up camp in the Home Depot lot a half a block from the RV place and next to the Brite Super Pharmacy.

They used one of those prefabbed display sheds as shelter. Their car was nearby, a firepit and their belongings were still there, probably just the way they left them.

They were inside the shed, both dead.

The second I saw them, I told Fleck to stay back. They may not have been deaders and a threat, but they were a threat to him nonetheless.

Their necks and arms showed they had the virus.

No bite marks whatsoever.

They were sick and they knew it. The male had a signal bullet wound to the head and she, evidently, had taken her own life.

They knew they were sick and knew what they would become.

They opted out. I didn't blame them.

It was what The Colony had told us about. How the virus mutated and was being carried somehow. Lev never knew how he caught it. I didn't need to be a scientist to figure out people spread it. It worked like a weapon. The virus was silent, it crept in without notice, without symptoms. Burying itself and wreaking havoc for days before it could even be detected on the early detection scanners.

The couple could have passed a checkpoint a week earlier, and been let through carrying the virus. How many people did they meet, come into contact with?

It was a scary thought.

After going through their things, I learned their names were Colt and Selma from Indiana. A picture with the dog confirmed she belonged to them.

I didn't have the heart to tell Fleck I found a dog tag with the name Marcy on it.

He wouldn't have changed it anyhow.

We checked out Brite Pharmacy for deaders, and Fleck, suggesting I keep his dog with me, left to prep the RV while I started the shopping list.

He would join me once it started charging.

The store was more than a neighborhood pharmacy, it had everything in it. The first thing I did was go immediately to the pharmacy and grabbed some medication I was familiar with.

It's strange how while in the store, I was suddenly seeing things we needed and either had used so much of or never had in the first place.

Cough syrup, allergy medicine, Calamine lotion. More diapers for the baby, batteries. I loaded up the cart as I browsed the aisle with a quiet Three Sixteen by my side.

It probably would be easier to bag all the items when I was done.

"Nila!" Fleck called out. "Where are you?"

I paused in grabbing an item and peered up to the sign. "Aisle Nine."

"RV's charging," he said with his voice moving closer. "Holy shit that cart is full. That was fast. How's it…ug."

"What?"

"You had to be in this aisle."

"What is wrong with this aisle?" I asked.

"It has…all this…you know."

"Seriously?" I laughed. "Considering there are three women in the cabin who menstruate, I would think this is an appropriate aisle."

Fleck turned his back as if being polite. "Just grab what you need."

That really made me laugh until we both heard the sound of it.

A bang. A loud bang followed by the crunching and banging sound of metal.

"What the fuck was that?" Fleck asked.

"I don't know."

The sound was steady and loud, growing louder each second. A mixture of metal smashing metal and metal scrapping concrete.

"It sounds like the movie *Transformers*," Fleck commented and walked toward the door.

We stepped outside and the sound was louder. We both turned left to right trying to see what was causing the noise. But we couldn't see.

"It's coming from that way." Fleck pointed.

"The highway?" I asked.

"Maybe."

"The highway is jammed. It can't be. I wish we could see."

"We can. Come on."

Moving at a good trotter's pace, Fleck headed in the direction of the RV Park and Storage with Three Sixteen keeping up the pace.

I didn't know what he was planning and didn't understand at first how he was going to see the highway. It was close to us, but it was up further on the hillside. All I could see was the guard rail.

Then it hit me what he planned to do.

At the very end of the lot, Fleck stopped at a huge tractor trailer. Using the outside ladder, he climbed up to the roof of the cab. "Come on," he called to me.

"Stay," I told Three Sixteen and climbed up the rungs.

At the top, Fleck reached down his hand to help me up and over.

I didn't think I'd be able to see anything.

Once I stood, I knew my thinking was wrong and the highway came into clearer view.

As crazy as the world had become, with what Fleck said, I wouldn't have been surprised to see a ten-story alien robot walking down the road.

What I did see was far worse. It made my stomach sicker than it already was.

It was a caravan. Large plow trucks lined up straight across the highway, moving at the same speed, pushing the cars that congested the road, smashing into them. Bulldozing to clear a drivable path for the long line of military trucks that followed.

SEVEN

WHAT TO EXPECT

Nila

It was the smallest RV on the lot, but once we moved it onto the property it really looked huge. Much bigger than the camper we had for Edi. We parked it south of the cabin, far enough away that it didn't shade the garden that Edi had started.

I thought a lot about the tiny houses on wheels, and how there was a place near Franklin, PA that had them. We had plenty of land, but with the military convoy that we saw headed north, leaving the area wasn't an option.

First priority was getting the RV back to the cabin along with all the supplies we had gathered. We gathered quite a bit after we stayed low, watching the trucks roll by us. It made me nervous because our cabin was north. But there were so many vehicles, I couldn't image them leaving the highway and was hopeful Big Bear Mountain wasn't their destination.

We decided after we brought everything inside, we would gather Ben, Bella, and Meg to let them know what we saw.

They were pretty enthusiastic about the RV. Bella and Meg immediately talked about moving in it together.

"Can I stay in there with the baby?" Bella asked. "Can I? Not that your cabin isn't nice, it is. But…"

"You guys can decide that," I told her. "Talk about it amongst yourselves, it really doesn't matter to me who lives in it."

As far as our new pet addition, Fleck was a little let down when Katie didn't get excited about it or give him a hard time. She hardly had a reaction.

Even when he said, "My dog is a much cooler zombie sniffer than yours."

She merely responded with, "We'll see about that," then took Caesar with her and walked away.

Fleck and I took the supplies inside and sorted them out. Stocking items under the floorboards and putting other things away in the cabinets.

I had grabbed a bunch of coffee when we were out, a lighter roast so maybe Ben wouldn't make it so strong.

After an hour, we asked if they would come in and we had them sit around the table to tell them about what we saw. I didn't know what to make of it or actually how I felt. Mainly because I didn't know what it meant.

They weren't all too surprised.

"We wondered what that sound was," Ben said. "It was in the distance. It sounded like something from an alien movie."

"See." Fleck snapped his finger. "I said the same thing. *Transformers.*"

"Yes, exactly." Ben nodded.

"What does this mean?" Bella asked. "I mean for us. Does it even affect us?"

I opened my mouth to answer. "Well—"

Then Meg spoke. "This is such great news. It really is. I just love hearing that."

"Why?" I asked. "It may be bad."

"You said it was military trucks, right?" she asked. "The military isn't a bad thing."

"I'm not saying it is, but rolling through, that many trucks, something is up," I said.

"Whatever it was," Fleck said, "the sound disappeared so they went really north."

"Well, it has to be good. Maybe it's The Colony," Meg said. "They lost Colony One. Maybe they're building another."

I chuckled. "Okay, that's not a good thing. It would be a horrible thing."

"Are you serious?" Meg asked. "The Colony was a good thing. People were safe."

"It fell."

"We made it out. I mean what did they do to you?" Meg questioned. "What did they do that made them so bad in your eyes? They're trying to rebuild the world."

"It's a breeding ground for that virus," I argued. "Lev would never have gotten sick if we hadn't been there."

Ben put in his two cents. "You don't know that, Nila, there were a couple days on the road after you evacuated from Colony One. He could have gotten it anywhere."

"So why didn't she?" I pointed at Meg. "She was with us. She isn't immune at all. If he got it on the road, why didn't she?"

Meg replied, "Maybe it's not as contagious as you think."

"Maybe…" I said snidely. "You need to go out there and look at the deaders that are in the woods, that come to the gate, that we find. No bite marks and fresh. That virus is out there again and stronger."

"You don't need to get so angry, okay?" Meg said. "I was just saying."

"I know what you were saying."

"Nila," Ben said my name with a slight hint of warning. "Let's not argue. Now…you saw this convoy. Were you two thinking of going to look for it?"

Fleck shook his head. "No, that never came up. I mean unless we want to see if they are a threat, they don't bother us, we don't bother them. So why would we?"

"To get rescued, maybe," Meg replied.

Hearing that just struck me the wrong way. "Rescued? Rescued, like you're being held captive here."

"That's not what I meant," Meg said. "I mean, yeah rescued, but to get us out, down from the mountain where we're safer."

With a "Ha," I folded my arms and spoke on edge. "Listen, no one is making you stay here. If you want to feel safer or get rescued, by all means leave. Get the fuck out." I stormed from the kitchen and out the backdoor. Briefly, I heard Ben calling for me, I guess trying to stop me. But I wasn't sticking around and I wasn't going to apologize for how I felt.

I made my way off the porch, really needing some air. I walked a bit and before I knew I was right there at our little cemetery.

Maybe subconsciously it was where I wanted to go.

I groaned out when I saw Lev's grave.

"Oh, man, Lev." I lowered to the ground. "I really am pushing the bitch zone." Closing my eyes, I reached for the dirt, gently moving it and imaging his voice.

"Nila, you know that is not a word you like."

"I know. I guess it's just been a weird day. We went to Cranberry to grab an RV to get some people out of the cabin. And we saw…we saw an entire military convoy traveling up seventy-nine, plowing their way through all the cars."

"Do you think they are The Colony?"

"Actually, yeah, I do. And that new woman sees nothing wrong with The Colony. I mean, Lev, if they are The Colony, what are they doing here?"

"It is a highway. Maybe they were just traveling through to somewhere else."

"Are they bad?"

"No, they have good intentions. They just do not handle things like we would like."

"Oh, my God, I just remembered. They like gunned down people for showing signs of the virus. They nearly gunned you down."

"But they did not."

"Still, they almost did. So they suck, Lev, they really suck. And Katie is just being stranger than usual. Her mouth is driving me nuts. She's so mouthy with Fleck."

"Then you need to talk to her and tell her."

"That is easy for you to say, Lev. You aren't…" I stopped when I heard the scuffling sound. Turning around some, I saw Ben. "Hey," I said to him.

"Hey. Sounded like you were having quite the conversation."

I stood. "I was. But…" I glanced back at the grave. "Think I'm crazy or seeing things. Maybe when I hit my head, but not now."

"It's your way of dealing."

"It's my way of trying to make it through this," I said. "He was my best friend. The one I always talked to, ended my day talking to. Now there's just this big empty space in my soul. I shouldn't feel as lost as I do."

"Why not?" Ben asked.

"Because I have my daughter still."

"That doesn't mean you can't grieve deeply for your friend. It'll take a while, Nila. If you need to talk to him, you do that."

"I miss him. I miss him so much. It's really affecting my moods, too."

"Like, how you were with Meg?" Ben pointed back toward the cabin.

"No. No, that had nothing to do with Lev. I was pissed."

"She's just naïve," Ben defended her. "After the outbreak she was fortunate to be in a survivor camp, then Colony One. She was never really out here. So of course, to her, this isn't survival."

"She needs to know how lucky she is to be here."

"I believe she does. You just have to understand her. You don't deal well with outsiders."

"I know. It doesn't help that I'm just sick. Nauseous all the time. Sometimes a little, sometimes I wanna just throw my guts up."

"Nila, you have a head injury," Ben said. "That will take time to heal."

"I know, but I also think it's something else."

"Like what?"

I lowered my head some, looking at Ben through the tops of my eyes. Then I spoke out loud the words that had rattled through my head after Katie handed me the cracker. "I'm...I think I might be pregnant."

"Wow. Are you sure? I mean, it really could be the head injury."

"No, I'm not sure. I did grab a test from the store today," I said. "But I'm almost three weeks late. I thought, you know, it was Lev's death, that made me late, but it was Lev."

"Nila, if you are, that's a bit of Lev that lives on."

"Yeah, yeah, I know."

He tilted his head and gave me a curious look. "Why do you sound so concerned?"

"Because I am."

"We will make sure you are fine. I'll make sure of it. Hey, look how we did with Christian when he was a newborn. We're kid kingdom on the mountain. We'll do just fine."

"That's not what I'm worried about."

"What is it?"

Arms folded tightly to my body, I spoke softly. "Ben, if I am pregnant, then I know exactly when I got pregnant."

"Okay."

"And knowing exactly when I got pregnant, I also know, there is a really good chance that Lev was already infected." I saw it on Ben's face. He tried to not show a reaction, but he did. His jaw flinched a little and he blinked a few extra times.

"Nila..."

"If he was infected, Ben...What does that mean for the baby?"

EIGHT

HIDE AND SEEK

Sean
July 19

This car was an older model, and I liked it much better than the previous one. It was the third one I had picked up, and I believed third time was a charm. It was going to get me where I was going.

I was on foot for nearly a day, but I was prepared. Once free and safe from Colony One, and confident that no one had followed me, I stopped at Grizzley Bear Sporting Center and picked up what I needed, which was everything but a canvas jacket as I already had one.

I grabbed a couple new backpacks, one more for hiking, a sleeping roll, and small camping supplies. When I did, I felt like my old self. The one that left his life behind and set out for the road.

Of course, I didn't have a choice, the outbreak and rise of the dead took away my choice to stay in my town.

It was too painful.

I never expected back then that I would live. Although I was a police officer, I wasn't some tough guy. I didn't deal with crime much. A wayward mouthy teenager or drunk was the norm. The dead were new territory for me. Then again, they were for everyone.

The impulse to kill them or put them down right away wasn't natural. They were people you knew and loved, and putting a bullet in their head when they were walking toward me was a nightmare.

I always suspected I would wake up one night in horrendous pain, finding myself the dinner plate for the dead.

But the will to live became my skill to live.

On my current journey I didn't worry about the dead so much. I took them out when they were a threat, I left them alone if they weren't.

The first car I had taken from the evacuation center didn't even get me out of Vermont.

Finding a replacement vehicle wasn't as easy as I thought. Too many people left their cars running, or they had sat too long without being started.

I resolved myself to walking and traveled on foot for an entire day, then I found the second car. It took me to Syracuse and provided me a safe place to sleep. It was strange, because I had heard so many stories of how Canada remained infection free and that Americans tried to flee there. But I never truly saw signs that Americans traveled in droves until I got to Syracuse.

There were signs everywhere. Hand painted signs that had names.

Marcus Lee was here and went to Canada.

Safe House if you are going to the border.

Things like that.

I wondered how many people made it, how many lived. There were rumors that farther north in Canada, they didn't have the undead.

But north was not my focus.

I'd walked another half a day when I found Betsy.

That's what I named the old tan car, like my father called his car Betsy.

"Come on, Betsy," he would say if the car slid in the snow or had issues. "Come on, Betsy, you can do it."

The car made me think of my father. He loved working on cars and hated when they got so computerized.

My Betsy would have been a classic had it been in pristine condition. Instead it had been used a lot. I suspected the odometer had been turned many times. Like my father, Betsy's owner was handy with cars and kept her running well. If she failed, in the trunk, just like my father had, was a toolbox and spare parts. Parts that could easily go on a trip. Belt, hose, plugs, he knew his car well.

I was curious when I saw the mass of emergency stuff in the trunk so I peaked in the glove box to find out the owner's name. Because the spare part thing was something my father did, I was hoping the owner's name was George, like my dad.

It wasn't.

It was Parker.

Parker was headed somewhere. He had survived the initial outbreak, that was evident. He had supplies, water, and a rifle in the car, along with two gas canisters.

Where was he going? Why did he just leave the car? Had he died? Maybe he ended up at The Colony.

The car was so old it still had an ashtray in it and the person that last drove it was a smoker. Smashed butts packed that ashtray. I liked the car, I liked Parker and I missed my father. I missed my family.

Driving Betsy had me drowning in thoughts while I listened to music Parker had in the car. Old songs, stuff my own dad listened to, and my thoughts took me to the last time I saw him.

It was a few weeks before everything really went insane, before we knew about the rising dead. How the infected went insane before they died and kept on going.

He had just gotten back from that senior singles cruise. He complained he didn't meet anyone and had caught a cold.

He was stuffy and congested and had this weird cough. I didn't worry much about it until he developed a fever.

Apparently, the doctors didn't worry either.

Go home. Rest. Plenty of fluids.

He did that. But got worse. Knowing what I know now, it was with the virus. He grew pale and gray. His veins were daker, almost black, and they were prominent on his neck and face.

My father felt agitated, and I became worried, it was so unlike him. I kept driving by his house every few hours, whether on shift or not, just to go in and check on him.

Then one day, his last day, I found him at the bottom of the stairs.

He had fallen, hit his head, and died.

He wasn't even supposed to be out of bed. But my father never turned, and for that I was grateful. Back then we didn't know about the dead rising. I really didn't know what I would have done if he had.

Within a week, everything erupted. Most of the town was ill, and days later it was chaos as they transformed from being sick in bed to mad lunatics, attacking everyone.

For me it started after I returned to duty from a week of bereavement. I was sitting at a light and my car was attacked.

It was a nightmare. It took two days and numerous attempts to get in touch with the national guard for all of us in my town to realize we were on our own. We would have to take matters into our own hands.

I didn't even want to think about how many people I put down, and they hadn't been at the dead phase.

Amazing how a car can not only transport you on a road, but through memories as well.

Betsy did just that.

Losing someone you love during the outbreak was a totally different grieving process. My father passed at the onset, there was still a funeral. I was able to grieve.

My brother was the next to go. He, like my father, had caught the virus, only my brother turned. He went into that 'rage' stage, still alive, moving on memory alone.

Like everyone else, I couldn't accept my brother was no longer in there. I even witnessed him hurting a woman, and like some gullible asshole, I called his name, pulling at him.

The woman's husband ended my brother's life. I couldn't 'feel' anger or sadness, only shock. As if because he turned, I wasn't permitted to hurt.

My children, however, were a different story. It wouldn't have mattered to me if they had torn apart the pope and eaten him for breakfast, it was soul crushing…grieving was a whole different thing.

They lived with my ex-wife, and when things started getting out of control, we all thought the best idea was to make a safe place for them.

Using firemen and local people, along with police officers as guards and protectors, the fire hall served as a camp.

Being ill informed about the virus and how it worked, it made us all vulnerable to defeat.

We no longer were going out and around the town, we stayed at the firehall just on the outskirts. We took shifts making a human wall of protection around the circumference of the hall, behind a hastily erected fence. We stayed dark, blackening out the windows, and we stayed quiet.

Although the dead and infected still gathered outside the fence. Nothing whatsoever was getting through us.

Nothing did.

It came from inside.

Because within days all news networks shut down, we didn't know about the domino effect. When one infected turned, many did, and as it happened in the firehall in the middle of the night, they dined upon the unsuspecting and sleeping people.

By the time the screams erupted, so many were dead or infected.

I was useless.

I kept my family by the door so they could easily escape, and it ended up being the worst place to be.

When I rushed in they were the first ones I saw. My ex-wife covered my nine-year-old son Garret's torn apart body, trying to protect him while two infected were tearing her to shreds. I could see the bones in her back, yet she held a protective hover.

Her eyes lifted to me. "Get the baby, Sean. Find the baby. Find the baby."

The baby. My god, my two-year-old daughter, Ava.

"Ava!" I screamed out over the gunshots and screams. Then I saw her. I heaved out a short-lived breath of relief when I saw her tiny little frame running, darting from the 'bad people' that came for her.

I could get her, I believed it.

But she ran right into them.

"No!"

I watched them encircle her, they were so fast, no matter what I did, they had her.

My baby didn't stand a chance.

Screaming with everything I had, I went ballistic. I swung out, I hit them, shot them. I didn't care if I got bit or infected, I wanted to be bit.

I couldn't bear to look at what they did to her. Her tiny bloody shoe was enough to devastate me to the point of no return.

The heartbreak, the pain is, was, and always would be real and strong. It causes your chest to hurt and stomach to flip every time the memory arises, and like a bad commercial it popped up all the time.

The emotional trauma was intense. I wanted to put a bullet in my head and say "fuck it." But if I did, and everyone who lost someone they dearly loved killed themselves, there would be no human race.

We'd all lost.

We all had insurmountable pain.

It was a different way to grieve. I carried my losses as a badge of inspiration to get the world back, to avenge their deaths by making sure others didn't die the same way.

Like with my family, I failed miserably.

Perhaps one day I wouldn't

Betsy was proving simply reliable. Sure, she used a bit more gas, but not only did I feel safe, the old body was like a tank, and plowed through four infected who had raced after me.

I hated doing it, but it was me or them.

However, that run-in left a slight mess on the windshield, and when I went to clear it, the windshield fluid pissed out the last drop and smeared the mess even more.

I drove a couple miles peeking through the streaks. After not seeing any deaders, I pulled over.

It was a roadside parking lot for one of those one-stop all places—store, gas station, diner—located just northeast outside of Eerie, PA. I didn't take any major roads, I knew traffic congestion would be bad.

I shut off the Don Henley song and the car. Complete silence engulfed me for the first time in hours.

After checking it was clear, I popped the hood, grabbed my rifle, then stepped out. I assessed the situation. No sounds, no movement, no smells.

There were a few cars in the lot, one at the pump—the driver probably didn't realize they didn't work without electricity. I was still good on gas and didn't need to add any, plus, I had a weird feeling about the place, I just wanted to hurry.

I made a comment in my mind about Parker, how he had everything good to go in the car except windshield fluid. I did recall seeing it in the trunk. Shouldering my weapon I retrieved it and carried it to the front of the car.

"Yeah, that's empty," I said, peering down into the container. I poured it in, enough to fill it halfway, then recapped the gallon bottle.

In case there was a leak in the fluid tank, I tossed the jug in the back seat. A leak was realistic since Parker was up on everything—there was no other reason for the empty washer fluid.

It was just when I was about to close the back door that I heard it.

It was like an electric shock sending my senses into instant alert and causing my heart to beat out of control.

I prayed it was my imagination.

It wasn't.

I heard it again.

A child's cry.

It was a young child, not quite a baby, but young.

"Jesus, no."

I pulled forth my weapon, shifted my body left to right, trying to hone in on the continuous cry.

Where? Where? Where?

I was caught in a dilemma. The child kept crying. What if I called to him or her, and it summoned the dead? Then again, what if the dead were around the child, and my voice would draw them back.

Time moved slowly, and finally I focused and discovered the direction of the cry.

It came from the diner.

Weapon ready I raced inside. It was an instant flashback to the night in the firehall.

I nearly tripped over the body of a man. It looked like a campsite had been set up inside the diner. A small hoard of maybe eight dead moved slowly around.

They bumped clumsily into tables but they were focused.

I didn't need to see to know what they were focused on.

A tiny little girl. So short and petite with dark hair, she had to be about two…the same age as my daughter had been.

If I wasn't thrown back into the nightmare before, I was now.

I was there watching my daughter again. However, this child stood a chance.

"Hey!" I blasted in my loudest voice. "Over here!"

They all turned.

It was good. That's what I wanted.

I waved out my arms, calling out, and then…the little girl cried.

Any attempt I made was countered by her crying. They decided they wanted her.

My insides screamed, "No!" and I raced forward. "Run, baby, run," I shouted.

They were close, edging in. I worried about shooting because I didn't want to take a chance on shooting her.

But she was just a baby, a toddler. She didn't know any better. All that poor baby knew was they were bad and scary. She wasn't listening to me, and then she did what any other child her age would do.

She crouched down, bringing her little knees to her face and she covered her eyes with hands barely big enough to hide her face.

To her she was hiding. If she couldn't see them, then surely they couldn't see her.

She was wrong, they saw her very well.

It wasn't going to happen again, not without me giving my all, even if it meant my life.

Many times I had heard the story about some person being so enraged, so impassioned, they only saw red.

I thought it was an expression, when in reality it really happened.

I literally saw red. Was it blood rushing to my eyes? Like a tinting filter over my vision, everything was red as I barreled forth.

Holding the rifle, I clobbered the three in the back, shoved another to the ground, then hands first I dove to the floor. Like a baseball player sliding headfirst into second base, my hands reached out, and instead of touching a base, I grabbed on to the huddled child.

I whipped her to me and into my fold.

Deader hands reached down, grabbing. I could feel the legs and arms against me, pulling my canvas jacket and jeans. I stood with an eruption of energy and in my best running back imitation, child cradled against my chest, I blasted through the hoard.

I didn't know the lay out of the diner, but running to the door wasn't an option. I'd have to run back towards the dead.

I made it to the kitchen before they did, and I hoped there were no more inside.

If there were, I didn't see them, and for safety, though probably not the smartest idea, I ran into the walk-in fridge.

I knew we'd be stuck there for a while, but I had to check her, see if she was hurt.

It was completely pitch black in there, and that caused her to cry even more.

"No, no," I said soothingly. "It's okay."

I knew there was always a flashlight or emergency light in a walk-in fridge, but I couldn't see it.

Just when I thought about opening the door for light, I heard the dead against it.

It took a few minutes of feeling around, baby crying in my ear, my hand running against slimy food, till I found it. It was one of those round push lights.

It wasn't bright, but it was enough light to find the flashlight.

"Please little one," I said. "Please don't cry. Please, I know you're scared. I know you are. I need to check you. Are you hurt? Are you crying because you're hurt?"

The little girl hyperventilated some, her mouth wide and distorted as she continued to cry.

I could only imagine what she was feeling.

She allowed me to sit her on a box, and using the flashlight I checked every single inch of her for a bite or scratch.

Once I saw she had nothing, I collapsed to the floor and couldn't move. I wanted to hug her, hold her. She didn't want held.

Instead, for an hour she called out, "Dada," causing the dead to be relentless.

Nonstop. She wouldn't have water or eat. Nothing would stop her calling for her dad. It was her cries feeding the moans of the dead, and the moans of the dead causing her cries. A relentless circle of noise.

Nothing soothed her.

I tried every father trick in the book.

Finally, like most babies, she cried herself to sleep. She exhausted herself so much that not even the pounding on the refrigerator door woke her.

Eventually, with me being quiet and her sleeping, the pounding stopped. I didn't hear them out there.

That didn't mean they were gone, they just weren't focused on the door.

I looked down at the time and knew it was getting dark out. We couldn't go anywhere.

After giving it some time, I pushed open the door slightly, not only to let fresh air in, but to see if they were still out there. They were. They meandered through the kitchen.

I shut us back in.

She woke up a lot calmer. She didn't have a verbal answer for her name, nor could she tell me how old she was.

I estimated her to be about two because of the way she spoke.

All night long I checked outside the door.

Finally, the dead moved on. At least out of the kitchen.

She understood enough of what I said to be still, and she was quiet.

We crept out of the refrigerator into the kitchen. Peeking over the counter into the dining room, I didn't see any there. The front door was open and it was light enough to let me know morning had arrived.

I was super cautious about making any noise, and looked everywhere. I could run from the dead; the infected were another story.

Once in the dining room, I spotted Betsy. She was still in the same spot, back door still wide open.

As I made my way to the door, I buried the girl's head in my chest. I didn't want her to see her father on the floor. At least I assumed it was her father.

Almost out, I saw the purple child's backpack next to a duffel bag. Balancing the child and rifle on my shoulder, I grabbed them both.

I moved at a slow pace, encumbered with everything. When I stepped outside, I saw the hoard.

It was like they sensed us and instantly turned our way.

Picking up the pace, I rushed as fast as I could to Betsy. I tossed the bags in the back, closed the door, and with the baby still in my arms, I jumped in the driver's seat.

The hoard of deaders were only five feet from us when I shut my door. Keys still in the ignition, I cranked the engine, shifted it into gear, and one handed, drove off.

I'd pull over and get things situated as soon as I knew we were clear.

At that moment I was so grateful, not only did we make it through the night, we made it out of there…alive.

NINE

LOOKING

Nila
July 20

"You've been quiet about it." Ben approached me from behind.

I didn't hear him coming. I was too busy watching Fleck divert his attention from checking the truck to looking for something elsewhere. He looked under the truck, then in the bushes. He wasn't saying anything, just looking.

It kind of amused me because we were supposed to be gone and on the road, yet he continued looking for something.

"What do you suppose it is?" was my reply to Ben.

"You're not."

Furrowing my brow, I turned to him. "I'm sorry, what?"

"I stated you've been quiet and you asked what I supposed it was."

"Oh, ah ... no. I meant, what do you suppose Fleck is diligently searching for?"

"He looks like he dropped something."

"Whatever it is," I said, "must be important. I wanted to get down to the Home Depot, then possibly Walmart."

"We need more stuff?"

"We're designing and building another outhouse. My father had the best one, I'm gonna make one better."

"Whatever gets you through the day," said Ben.

"True." I glanced at him. "I'm not … what?"

"Did anyone ever check you for attention deficit disorder?" Ben asked. "Because the way you switch gears in a conversation really can be maddening. I won't get mad if you actually have a disability."

"I'm sorry."

"Let's start again," Ben said. "You've been quiet about it."

"It meaning…?"

He raised his eyebrows.

It took a second, then I got it. "Oh, yeah, I have been. Sorry. Just embarrassed about telling you. I thought I was before I knew for certain."

"No need to be. We all make mistakes," Ben said. "Many women have done that. So how are you feeling?"

"It's only been a couple days, and I'm still sick."

"I told you it was the head injury." Ben waved his finger.

"No, it's the pregnancy."

"But you said you weren't pregnant."

"No, I didn't."

"Yes, Nila, you did," Ben argued. "You said you were embarrassed about it because you said something before you knew."

"Exactly."

"God damn it, Nila, quit talking in circles. Are you or aren't you?"

"I am."

Ben exhaled loudly. "Okay, now we need to come up with a plan to keep you healthy. I'm taking it you took the test."

"Yes, and I was actually going to talk to you and show you." I reached into my back pocket and pulled out the white test. "Clear as day. Pretty fast. Positive. See?" I extended it to him.

"Nila," he said calmly. "I really don't want to hold that."

"Oh, okay." I put it back in my pocket. "You saw though. Positive."

"I did," Ben answered. "But tell me why you put it back in your pocket?"

"Because I don't want to throw it away. What if someone finds it. We burn trash."

"How long do you expect to hide it?" Ben asked.

"I'm not hiding it. I'm just not ready for you to tell people. I will."

"Well, if that thing falls out of your pocket, you may have to tell them before you're ready."

"I'll throw it away inconspicuously when we go to Home Depot."

"That's just ridiculous," Ben said. "But whatever works. I will want to do an ultrasound on you in the next few weeks. So tell them before that because you'll need Fleck to go get the machine."

"I will. Would you feel slighted if I told you at this moment, I'm not really sure I'm comfortable with you giving me an internal?"

"We'll cross that bridge when we get there." Ben upped his chin. "Here comes Fleck."

"Hey." I clapped my hands together once. "You ready?"

"Have you seen Three Sixteen?" Fleck asked.

Ben chuckled. "You lost your dog already?"

"Dude, that's not even funny. I let her run about the yard, now she's gone," Fleck said.

"Oh, she's back by the chicken pen with Katie and Caesar," I said. "They went back there about fifteen minutes ago."

"You saw me looking," Fleck said. "Why didn't you say anything?"

"You didn't say you were looking for your dog. You looked under the truck for crying out loud," I argued. "For all I knew you were looking for your phone."

"You're the only crazy person who still carries your phone."

"For pictures, Fleck, pictures."

Fleck nodded. "Pictures."

"Alright," Ben interrupted. "Now that you two have argued, why don't you get going so you can get back here and start that outhouse. Why you're building another, I don't know."

"We need more than one bathroom around here," Fleck replied. "I'm thinking men's room, ladies' room."

Ben nodded. "Whatever you want. I'm going to round up the kids and work with them. Meg and I decided we need to start teaching them."

"While you're teaching them," Fleck said, "can you teach Katie to leave my dog alone."

"How about I do that, after I teach you how to share." Ben turned and started to walk away.

"And ask her …" Fleck yelled. "Why she has my dog in the chicken pen?" He then glanced to me. "Do you know why?"

"I haven't a clue. I'll find out though." I walked to the truck.

"Did you make a list?"

"Found my father's outhouse plans, so yeah, list already made. I copied it." I patted my back pocket. When I did I felt the test and made an instant reminder to myself to be careful pulling out the list. I opened the truck door and climbed inside.

"You think it will take long to get all the stuff?" Fleck asked once inside.

"Probably more time at Walmart," I replied.

"What are we getting from there again?"

"Clothes. Katie in this past year has outgrown all her clothes. I gave Addy's clothes to Maura, and Sawyer needs some things as well."

"Christian, too."

Once we pulled out of the gate, Fleck got out, secured it, and got back in. We drove down the winding road, but at the bottom he made a right instead of a left.

"Why are you going this way?"

"Okay, so hear me out. I hope you're okay with this. I've been doing a lot of thinking."

"About?"

"That convoy we saw. What do you say we go to Big Bear, grab some gas stash, top off the tank, and head north on seventy-nine?"

"You mean look to see if they're close?" I asked.

"Just to see if they're close," Fleck replied. "They cleared a path. They could be long gone."

"It's been a couple days."

"Exactly."

"How far north?" I asked.

"Not far. Twenty miles. That's it. If they aren't in a twenty-mile range, I'm not worrying. What do you say?"

"I think that's a really great idea. It will put my mind at ease. Because to be honest, I was thinking about them too."

"That's what I thought."

I truly did believe it was a good idea. I wasn't worried about what we'd find. A part of me believed they were just passing through.

What worried me more was how I would handle Big Bear. More than I wanted to admit, I was nervous about what kind of feelings it would stir up.

Walking back onto Big Bear property would be stepping into Lev's world, and I really wasn't sure I was ready for that yet.

TEN

NEARLY THERE

Sean
July 20

We had become buddies. That wasn't to say she hadn't called out for her father with questions numerous times, but she started to trust me.

Once we had left the diner, she did not like driving in the car on my lap. Which left me with a predicament.

How was I supposed to drive in the car at all with the baby?

The car only had lap belts and that wouldn't suffice for someone as pint-sized as her. I needed a car seat or something. I made it about ten miles, wondering in my mind if going to a store in Erie would be the best choice or chance to take, or if I should turn around.

Which would be safer?

It was only ten miles so I turned around.

The hoard had made it down the road, following us I suppose. I zipped around them, causing the baby to cry and I made it back to the parking lot.

One of those cars had to belong to her father. I just couldn't see him walking with her.

They had belongings, maybe they lived on the road, but to walk with a baby was dangerous, especially with so many cars everywhere.

The car at the pumps drew my attention, it was slightly cleaner than the others. I pulled right alongside and, carrying the baby, I looked inside.

Sure enough, my instincts were correct.

In the front passenger was a car seat.

As a police officer with the reputation for most vehicular citations, I would have been all over that car seat in a pre-outbreak world.

It was in the front seat, it was for an older child and the baby was way below the weight for that.

Still, it would do. I retrieved it and placed it in Betsy.

At first, I placed it in the back seat, but Betsy didn't have harnesses and I would have to loop the seatbelt over. Then just as I was about to put her in it, I saw the hoard slowly returning.

My paternal instincts trumped the lawman in me.

I strapped her in, then lifted the car seat, putting it in the front and buckling her down.

I wanted her near me, like her father did, in case of trouble.

After an hour of driving, watching her little feet kicking told me she had calmed down a lot.

"Are you hungry?" I asked. "Eat?"

She shook her head. I was going to dismiss her nodding, then I remembered my own daughter, how she didn't know yes from no. I was so nervous and cautious about having her in my car, I pulled over and stopped so I could reach in my bag for a cracker.

When I handed it to her, she thanked me.

In my short time with her, I realized her vocabulary was limited. She knew thank you and dada, and surprisingly potty.

She didn't know her name, and I couldn't keep calling her child or baby, so I named her, June, after the diner where I found her, Juniper's Grill.

I thought about her father a lot. How badly I felt for him, and how outstanding of a job he did. Whether or not June was his birth child, he had taken care of her. She wasn't malnourished that I could see, her coloring was good.

He had done a great job.

What happened? How did a man go a year, diligently taking care of a baby, to suddenly get attacked by the dead?

Like many times I have seen, and because of where he was, I was willing to bet it happened when he slept.

They just didn't get June because they didn't see her.

But I would never know what happened to her father. God willing if I survived long enough for her to ask, I would tell her he died protecting her.

Because he did.

And I vowed from that moment, for the sake and memory of my own children, for my shortcomings in saving them, and for June's father, I would protect her at all costs.

Like I hoped someone would have done for my child.

I was curious what was in the bags I'd grabbed. I assumed some clothing, though not diapers because June impressively didn't need them.

Then again, I probably wouldn't want to change diapers in the apocalypse either.

I was fairly sure we were close to our destination, but I needed to pull over and figure it out. Plus, June needed a break from the car and I wanted to search those bags.

After finding a great hideout in a shed, I hid the car to look like it was abandoned and then unloaded it. It took a bit to carry the bags because I always had one arm full with June. I set up a little area for the afternoon break, laying a blanket on the floor, lighting an LED lantern and giving June some food.

There were no dead in the area, at least none I saw, and I felt it was safe. But even so I blocked the door.

In the purple child's backpack there were fresh clothes for June, but I found something I was lacking in the larger bag.

A map.

In a world of electronics and GPS, maps were a thing of the past. It used to be that any convenience store had them. And I wasn't thinking when I was at the sporting good's store. I was too focused on making ground.

"What do we have here," I said to June as I spread out the map. "Let's see if I'm close or we're close. Here's where we are." My finger touched the map. "And here … oh. Look, June, we are close. Really close. See here? You know what this says?" I asked, as if she understood me. "Big Bear. You see that? Big Bear."

"Big Bear Mountain," Nila said to me the second night we went out shooting after she had come to Colony One.

"What in the world is Big Bear Mountain?"

"Pennsylvania. In Butler, you're probably not familiar with that."

"I've heard of Butler County."

85

"That's it," she said. "And it's not technically Bear Mountain. I really don't think the mountainside has a name." She shrugged. "People started calling it Big Bear because of the campsite. Lev's father started it decades ago."

"Big Campsite?" I asked.

"Gave KAO a run for their money. It was a good one."

"So that's where you were all this time? Not Florida."

"Not at the campsite. More like my father's property and cabin, it shared a property line with Big Bear. We had all we needed to survive there, you know, well water, a flourishing garden."

"So why did you leave?" I asked.

"We all thought for the sake of the kids we should see what else was out there. So …we ventured south," she said. "And we're headed north again. Lev never wanted to leave."

"I wouldn't want to leave either," I told her.

"Every time I think of it, I really didn't want to leave. What about you?"

"Me, after my town fell, I was just a nomad until I came here."

"Which did you like better?" she asked.

"Don't get me wrong. I love what The Colony is doing and what they stand for," I told her. "But there has to be something simpler out there. There has to be."

"Big Bear," June said, pointing.

"Good girl. That's right. And here is where we are. We're not far. Not far at all."

If I was correct, I was on target. The map clearly showed the Big Bear Campsite. The wooded area wasn't named at all, and Nila's cabin had to be somewhere in the vicinity.

Was Nila there? I wasn't a hundred percent sure. The fragment of voice on the radio sounded like her, but it was just a snippet.

Even if Nila wasn't there, the fact that she said it had well water and a garden was reason enough to try to find it.

It had been a year since the outbreak and canned foods and box goods were reaching their expiration dates. While Meals Ready to Eat and other survivor food had a good shelf life, I had to look beyond that. I had June, I wasn't alone now. There was a new focus for me.

Stability.

And from what Nila briefly described, her father's grounds would be perfect.

ELEVEN

FOUND

Nila

Just shy of the twenty miles intended, Fleck and I traveled eighteen miles north. We hadn't seen a single truck. We even stopped to listen.

No noises.

I felt the pause in traveling to evaluate the quiet helped with the motion sickness. My anxiety over seeing the military movement began to leave. We deducted they were probably headed back toward Vermont and to Colony One.

The research facility was there and still standing. I couldn't imagine they'd abandon that even if they moved their scientists. They couldn't have moved their research.

After talking in the truck we both deducted it was post-Colony paranoia, along with what happened in Cobb County.

They were looking for us then, so it was safe to assume they were looking for us now.

Although, Fleck came up with a counter argument to that. The Colony had tested both Katie and I and got all that they needed from us.

I found some comfort in that reasoning.

I didn't want to run, I just wanted to figure out a way to make life better and safe at the cabin. Safe and long term.

"Not sure I can agree with you," Fleck told me.

"I don't understand. It has everything we need."

"You sound like Lev. We have four kids, is that enough for them? Only having each other?"

"What are you suggesting?" I asked. "We find a community? Fleck, it's dangerous right now. With the dead, the virus."

"I know. But Nila, I don't want to be alone the rest of my life. I don't."

"That's weak."

"How is that weak? Just because you could care less either way, I do. I thought I had a chance with Chandy."

"Fleck, you knew her for like five seconds."

"Still," he said. "It was a companionship I hadn't had in a year."

"What about Meg?" I asked.

"What about her?"

"She's like your age. Hit on that."

"Hit…on that?"

"Yeah." I shrugged. "You want companionship, she's perfect."

"Come to think about it, she's not bad."

"No, a little bossy. But you say I don't talk to anyone, you don't either. Bet if you strike up a conversation with her, it goes better than you think."

"Maybe I will. Just don't put any good words in for me with her, because there's this cat fighting thing happening between you two."

I laughed at that. It was funny.

We arrived at what was supposed to be our only destination, the Home Depot. We slowly made our way through the parking lot, making sure we didn't call attention to deaders. We didn't see any, which was always a good sign. With the amount of noise the military trucks made, it probably drew every deader in a twenty-mile radius.

We didn't see any large hoards.

They had to be out there.

They always followed noise.

"You got that list?" Fleck asked, putting the truck in park and opening the door.

"Yep." I stepped out.

He walked immediately to the door, holding out his hand. "Can I see it?"

I pulled it from my pocket as I walked and extended it.

"Why do you have a toilet seat on here."

"Because it will make it look nice, like the one my dad built," I replied.

"See I thought we were building a simple outhouse."

"We can, if you want to do that men's room, women's room thing. Build a simple one for you guys all you want."

"You sure this amount of wood?"

"I copied directly from my father's list."

"And there's a saw?"

I nodded as we approached the door. "Lev had one at the cabin, it's in the…" I slowed down. "Shed."

"What is it?"

"What if we cheated?" I asked.

"With what?"

"What if we took one of these smaller prebuilt sheds and used it as an outhouse, then the only thing we'd have to build is the toilet part itself over the hole."

"That's actually not a bad idea," Fleck replied. "Only problem with that is getting the thing on the truck. We can grab a prefab kit."

"The lawn mower one," I stated. "It's smaller and we'd just need the wood for the bum box."

"The…bum box." Fleck laughed. "You know what else. Little houses instead of trailers. We could figure out how to make these tiny homes."

"Why not?"

We talked about the tiny house thing a lot while we shopped in the store. It was hard to see the list in the dark, but I was confident after nearly an hour in there we had gotten everything we needed.

Fleck had made two trips with wood to the front door, then on the third trip he balanced the board as he walked out with me.

I followed behind with the cart, but without the really cool marble toilet seat and paper roll holder.

I nearly bumped into him when he stopped cold. "What is it?"

"Look at that. A pregnancy test on the ground."

My eyes widened.

"Man, some poor sucker is pregnant. I feel bad for her." He continued to the truck.

"Why?"

"Who wants to have a baby in this world?" He placed the wood in the bed. "I mean, it's a dinner bell, right? The dead would snatch it right up."

"You don't know that."

He slid the wood in. "They follow sound. They'd hear that thing cry all night long."

"Christian didn't. We kept him safe," I said.

"That was luck." Fleck turned to head back to the store. "Just unload the light stuff," he instructed. "I'll be right back."

I disagreed with him. But had to ask myself, would I have disagreed if I wasn't the one pregnant? Just as I started unloading the stuff, Fleck hurried back to the truck, giving me the 'be quiet' sign of his finger to his lips.

"What?" I whispered.

Quietly, Fleck opened the passenger door, reached in, and grabbed his ice pick. He then pulled his revolver out.

He had seen something.

I followed suit and grabbed my weapons.

Staying close, I followed Fleck a few feet across the lot. He stopped and pointed to a small blue shed.

He raised his ice pick as the door slowly opened.

Surely he was prepared for deaders to come out, but the second the door opened, I reached up and lowered his hand.

"It's not the dead," I said in shock, walking to the shed.

"Nila," Fleck called my name in a whisper.

"It's not the dead," I repeated.

I came to a dead stop in shock when I saw him emerge slowly from the shed holding a baby.

If I wasn't mistaken, it was Sean from The Colony. His hair was slightly longer, and he had a beard. He wasn't dressed in any Colony military garb, and the baby on his arm replaced the rifle I was used to seeing him with.

"Nila." Sean smiled. "I thought I heard you."

"Oh my God," I said. "Sean."

Fleck looked confused when he tapped me on my shoulder. "Who?"

I was full of questions, especially since the last time I saw Sean was at Colony One as we were evacuated.

"I didn't know if you were alive or dead," I said to him. "How did you end up here?"

"You," he said. "The one night you told me all about your camp and Big Bear."

"I remember that."

"Um…" Fleck stepped forward, lifting a finger. "One thing. How did you know we'd be here or even alive?"

"I didn't," Sean answered. "To be honest when I knew I was going to split from The Colony, this is where I thought to go. You said it was self-sufficient."

"So, you were just gonna take her land?" Fleck asked.

"Fleck," I scoffed.

"What? Where's he been?"

"I was cleaning up and recovering bodies at Colony One," Sean said. "Honestly, it was my intent to come here. I hoped you guys were here, but it was my destination."

"Is the baby from Colony One?" I asked.

"No, I found her. Now she's my buddy."

"So sweet." I reached out and touched her tiny fingers. "You're a sweetie, what's your name?" I asked.

"She doesn't know it," Sean answered. "I call her June."

"Such a pretty name. Such a pretty little girl." I upped my voice. "Aren't you sweetie. And brave."

"Oh my God," Fleck scoffed.

"So is everyone with you?" Sean asked. "Everyone fine?"

"You mean her daughter?" Fleck asked. "That's what you want to know."

"Fleck, stop," I told him. "We all are fine except Lev. He ended up with the virus and didn't make it."

"I'm very sorry."

"Me too."

"Alright," Fleck said. "We came here to get stuff for the second outhouse. We need to do that, get the shit loaded into the truck."

"Here, if you don't mind…" Sean handed me June. "I'll help."

"I don't mind." I took the baby.

Fleck moved his hand in a half assed wave for Sean to follow him. Walking toward the store, Fleck scuffed his foot on the ground, kicking the pregnancy test. "Fucking test, who leaves a piss stick on the ground?"

Suddenly, Fleck had turned miserable. I didn't believe it was because he was threatened by Sean, but more so he didn't trust Sean for some reason.

I understood, but I trusted him. There was no reason not to.

Fleck was antsy the entire ride back to the cabin. He kept switching his hands on the wheel, shifting in his seat, and looking in the rearview mirror to Sean who followed us.

"He has a baby with him, Fleck. Why are you having such a hard time with this?"

"Just because he rescued a baby doesn't make him a good person. Don't you think it's a little strange he shows up right after we see all those military vehicles?"

"I would if I hadn't told him all about this place. He was in a shed with a baby."

"So you really think that takes away suspicion?"

"Yes."

Fleck nodded.

"I think you should trust him. Trust me," I said.

"Okay. What would Lev think right now?"

"What is it with you all the time asking me what Lev would believe?"

"Just curious because you sort of listened to him."

I laughed. "Lev would argue that I never listened to him, but he would say…"

I glanced out the window, thinking about that.

"Nila," Lev would say. "I think the guy is an asshole and we are making a mistake letting him into our home."

"Well?" Fleck asked.

"Lev would say to give him a chance."

Fleck laughed. "Lev also said to check out that RV. He had as much of a bad gut instinct as…what the fuck?"

I was too busy looking at Fleck to notice, but when he switched up what he was saying, I glanced out the windshield.

Immediately, I grabbed my pistol when I saw the deader sauntering toward the gate.

A gate that was open.

"Fuck." Fleck stopped the truck, reached down for my crowbar, wound down the window, and hit the gas.

As we flew up the remaining distance, he leaned out the window and nailed the deader with the crowbar, nearly losing control of the truck.

We swerved as we went through the gate, narrowly missing it when we pulled on to the property.

With an "Oh my God," I flung open my door the moment Fleck stopped the truck.

Five deaders were on the porch, while one kept trying to make it up the steps. It was as if they just didn't have the strength to pull themselves up. His foot kept slipping. The others moved sluggishly, their hands slowly smacking the windows.

The interior shutters were closed, which told me Ben had everyone inside, hatched down.

They didn't notice us standing there, nor did they turn when Sean pulled up next to the truck.

"Did we leave the gate open?" I asked Fleck.

"No, I'm sure we closed it."

Sean stood on the other side of Fleck. "There are no others back there. Should I shut the gate?"

"Yeah." Fleck lifted the crowbar.

"Wait," I told him. "There are no others out there. Why don't we lead them from the property? Lead them out and when they approach the gate take them out that way."

"Why don't we just take them out now? They're slow," Fleck said. "And useless. Nelly on the steps is an easy out. No reason not to put them down here."

"Yeah, there is. There are kids in there. Do you want to clean up a deader mess?" I asked. "Those are old deaders, too, they'll be really nasty."

Fleck turned to me, his jaw twitched in thought and he exhaled. "Okay. Sean, move the car with the baby. I'll call them to the gate, have them chase me, once they're through, shut the gate and call them back. I'll make my way back in."

"No," I said. "I'll lure them. I know the property better than anyone. And…" I took the crowbar. "This is mine."

Sean quietly got in the car and inched it to the other side of the truck, out of the path of the deaders. Once he was clear, I whistled and shouted gaining their attention.

The deader on the step turned first, and fell, then the others caught my shouting and followed. They came down the stairs, trampling over the one that had fallen.

Fleck and I kept yelling and sure enough they followed, slowly.

It seemed to take forever, and I even had to move closer to them to keep their attention. I kept thinking if all deaders were like them, there would be no danger. They were, for lack of a better description, clearly dying off.

I drew them closer to the gate, and Fleck broke off. "What are you doing?" I asked. "They're gonna follow you."

"No they aren't. That mother fucker is making me nervous."

I was just about to ask "who," thinking it was a bad time to get on Sean, until I saw him go to the deader on the ground.

One strike down and Fleck put the ice pick in his head. "I'll clean it. I promise."

I shook my head, walking backwards, drawing the four remaining my way. I crossed through the open gate, verbally beckoning them to come get me. Once they cleared the fence and were coming for me in the driveway, Fleck shut the gate. Immediately, he started banging on the chain links and making a ruckus.

Feeling a slight victory when they turned back and headed to Fleck, I ran about fifteen feet down the road and veered to my right.

I wanted to hurry and circle around back to the fence. I knew it wouldn't take Fleck long to put them down. They would be clinging to the fence, and easy targets.

Confident, I spun around, never expecting to see a deader as she emerged from the tree line.

Because she startled me I screamed, and as she gasped with a wide mouth and swinging arms, I wailed the crowbar to the side of her head.

I really didn't have much luck putting them down with one strike. She titled and swayed and it took two more hits before I penetrated the skull enough for her to fall.

I had to jam the end of the crowbar downward to finally kill it.

Slightly out of breath and not seeing more ahead of me, I walked back to the fence. I didn't hear them yelling anymore, that told me it was done.

As I came up the crest toward the fence, Fleck was walking my way.

"You alright?" he asked. "I heard you scream."

"One jumped out and scared me."

"I hate when that happens."

"Me, too. Everything done?" I asked.

"All down."

"Good job," he said.

"You, too. I wonder what happened?"

"We'll find out. I feel like shit. I keep thinking we left the gate open."

"Well, Ben had the cabin shuttered. He had everyone inside."

We arrived back at the gate. Sean held June center of the yard, and as Fleck shut the gate and locked it, Ben emerged from the house.

Katie flew out from behind him, both dogs in tow, running to me. She paused and looked at the deader on the ground and made a sound of disgust. Immediately she ran and clung to my legs.

"Are you alright, sweetie?" I asked.

"Caesar and Three Sixteen warned us," Katie said. "So we had time to get in. They were super slow."

"Yes, they were." I ran my hand over her head and looked up as Ben approached.

"Newcomers?" Ben asked, pointing to Sean and June. "Where'd you find them?"

"At Home Depot," I replied. "You probably don't recognize him, but this is Captain Marshall. He helped us evacuate from Colony One."

"Aw, yes." Ben nodded and shook his hand. "Forgive me for asking, but how are you here?"

Sean pointed at me. "She told me about the place."

Ben nodded.

"Ben?" I questioned. "What happened? How did the dead get through?"

Ben groaned out in frustration. "The gate was wide open."

"Fuck." Fleck swung out his hand. "Fuck. We're sorry, Ben, we really are."

"No need," Ben said. "It wasn't you who left it open."

I was about to ask who it was, then I looked around. Our group was mainly children, other than Ben, only one other person in our camp was tall enough to open that gate and she wasn't there.

"Meg?" I asked.

"Yep." Ben nodded. "What else is missing?"

I glanced around and didn't see it. "Shit. Your station wagon."

"You got it. She took it," Ben said. "Her and her kid…are gone. They left. Along with a boat load of our supplies."

TWELVE

STRANGER

Sean

When I was seventeen, I started dating this girl. We went to her house after school to do homework. We were sitting in the family room, books open when her parents not only started arguing, the police showed up and arrested her mother on drug charges.

It wasn't a normal situation...ever. I can recall saying to her, before the police came, "Maybe I should leave?"

That feeling of being the third wheel, at the wrong place, at an embarrassing time, intruding in a family's private moment...that was how I felt stepping into the cabin and watching Nila throw a mild tantrum as she opened cabinets, closets, and even a hatch on the floorboard.

"At least she didn't take anything from here." Nila slammed the floor hatch shut and tossed a rug over it. "Do we know how much she took?"

"Enough," Ben replied.

"Unbelievable. Do you know when she left?"

"No," Ben said. "I thought her and her daughter were in the camper. I was in here with Katie and Sawyer. We were going over schoolwork. Three Sixteen was shoving against the door and Caesar was barking. I looked out and saw the dead. I yelled for Bella and Meg. Only Bella came from the RV and we hunkered down here. I didn't want to take a chance leaving the kids and taking them out. They weren't that big of a threat out there. They were older ones, been deaders awhile."

Nila shook her head with disgust and looked to the young girl holding a toddler younger than June. "Bella," Nila said to her. "You lived in the RV with her. Did she say anything to you?"

"She said you didn't want her here, that was it," the teenage girl replied.

"Well, I could care less either way, but her daughter shouldn't be out there," Nila said. "Didn't you notice when she left?"

"I thought she was coming to the cabin."

"And you didn't notice...I don't know, that she took and packed a ton of shit?"

"Nila," Ben interjected. "None of this is Bella's fault. Even if she did know, you can't blame her."

"I'm not," Nila defended. "I just find it hard to believe Bella didn't know."

"None of us did," Ben said. "She took a lot of stuff."

Fleck huffed. "Unbelievable. Now we have to replenish. Can't we go like one week without shopping. Why would she do this?"

"Mommy told her if she didn't like it," Katie said, "to get the—"

"Okay, alright," Nila cut her off. "I remember." She brought her hand to her head. "I don't know which to feel, guilty or pissed. Or...probably both."

I stood there listening, wondering if it were even my place to say anything. Figuring the worst that would happen was they would say to mind my own business, I decided to speak up. "Look, I don't know her. I don't. But I do know the traits of people that pack up and leave camp in the middle of the night, stealing supplies. They don't do it on a whim. It's on their mind for a couple of days. If the decision to leave is last minute, they take what they can grab. Sounds to me like she took a lot more than a handful of items. Do you know what all she took? Was it food only?"

Ben answered, "Haven't checked the back shed for supplies. It was food. Not sure how much. We'd have to really look to see if she took supplies. But she did"—he cringed looking at Nila—"Take one of the rifles from the closet. I went to grab one off the rack and noticed it was…"

Before he could finish, Nila brushed by him, and walked down a hall. I couldn't see what she was doing, but she blurted out a loud, "Fuck," before storming back.

"She took my father's 1982 Smith and Wesson Eastfield. I'm killing her. That was my father's. I want that back. I will get it. I'll find her after the deaders get her and pull it from her cold dead hands."

"Oh, Nila," Ben scolded. "Stop. That's a bit extreme and over the top even for you."

"The cold dead hand thing," Fleck said. "John Wayne, right?"

"Bite your tongue," she snapped. "It was Charlton Heston."

"Who?" Fleck asked.

Ben breathed out slowly to keep his patience. "Not everyone had a father like you, Nila, who talked about those guys. Listen, she took the rifle, I get that your mad."

"Won't do her any good. She'll have a false sense of confidence," Nila said.

"Why?" I asked. "Did the rifle not work?"

Nila chuckled. "It worked, she just took the sixteen gauge shells for the Old Browning instead of the twelve."

Fleck looked at me as if to explain. "Nila's father has a lot of classic rifles, if that's what you want to call them."

"So she had time to take food and at least a weapon?" I asked. "Along with the car, I'd say she had that packed or was packing for a couple of days."

"Here's my concern," Ben said. "And I know, Nila, you don't care."

"I do."

"Not just because she took your stuff," Ben continued. "My concern is Meg did not strike me as very survival savvy. The woman was at The Colony for a while. What makes her think she can just take off and be alright?"

Nonchalantly, and speaking so matter of fact, Katie said, "She wanted to find the rescue. You wouldn't let her be rescued Mommy."

Instantly, Nila looked at me. "We weren't keeping her hostage."

"I didn't think you were," I replied.

"Kid doesn't have a filter," Fleck stated. "But she's right. Not that we wouldn't let her be rescued, but Meg made that comment about getting rescued. She was calling out on the radio. Maybe she thinks there's something better out there and close by."

"But what?" Nila asked. "And where?"

Katie replied to that. "The people she talked to. But don't worry, Mommy, she didn't tell them where we were, like you did with the bad people last year that shot Lev and broke his leg."

"Gee thanks," Nila said. "Did you hear her? Did they tell her where they were?"

Katie shook her head. "No. But I bet she went to find them, Mommy. They're close. Listen." In a strange move, Katie stood from the couch and walked to the door.

"Katie, where are you going?" Nila asked.

"To see." Katie opened the door.

"See what?"

As soon as Nila asked that, I heard, they heard, the faint sound of a helicopter. It grew louder.

Without a second of hesitation, Fleck dove forward, grabbed Katie and pulled her back away from the door.

"Stay back," Ben instructed Nila who was about to step out. "I'll check. You and Katie stay out of sight." He stepped through the door, and I immediately followed.

It took for us both to step out into the yard to see the chopper, high in the sky and in the distance. It wasn't circling, it was just flying straight, as if to a destination.

I had been holding my breath for the few seconds I saw it in the sky. It moved on, the sound of it fading quickly. "At least it's not close," I said.

"If there's a helicopter right now in these parts." Ben looked at me. "It's close enough."

THIRTEEN

A LATE RETURN

Nila
July 29

My hopes were high it would be this day. For some reason, I was fine, until the morning after Meg had left, and suddenly I was hit with this feeling of guilt, thinking about her daughter, that poor child out there with someone who had very little skills on how to protect her.

We could have all been wrong about it. Maybe Meg was some sort of apocalypse survival queen, but could we take that chance with the life of her child?

We'd set a search limit.

Ten days.

We were about to go out for day nine.

Sean had a map with public landmarks and restaurants. Not that I didn't know the area, but it brought to attention some places to check.

Heck, I even went up to Big Bear to check there because maybe she was thinking it was a viable place.

I wished I hadn't gone.

I saw the source of a lot of the dead.

How that many even got there I couldn't figure out. Thankfully, we didn't pull the car all the way into Big Bear, so the deaders never followed us.

We knew we also had to think she may have actually gone beyond where we searched.

I didn't feel that was the case, but I felt responsible to check. Plus, what else was there to do? We were able to pick up items during every search to prepare for winter even though it was still some time away.

Me, personally, I had to think about things for the baby. God willing, all went well, and Ben saw no reason for it not to, the baby would be born in March, just at the end of winter. Pennsylvania weather was strange, March often brought a ton of snow.

Ben was still the only one who knew I was pregnant, him and Lev. I knew Lev wouldn't say anything. I was the only one who talked to him. I'd be lying if I said I didn't wish Katie's special abilities extended to talking to those beyond. I would be having her tap into Addy, my father, my brother, and Paul. Of course Lev, but for some reason I talked to him anyhow. He seemed to be the one person whose spiritual response I could sense.

Though I certainly questioned my own sanity at times. But my conversations with Lev got me through the day.

Sean commented once when he saw me taking my stroll, probably looking totally irrational talking to myself. When I explained, he likened it to a form of prayer. Not that I was praying to Lev, but I was reaching out for answers.

In a way that was right. I did reach out to Lev for answers.

It was almost time for our morning pow wow to talk about where we'd go look and why. While everyone finished their breakfast, I wandered outside to take a walk.

Eating in the morning still didn't agree with me, but by early afternoon, I could eat anything.

Outside in the yard, the behavior of our dogs grew more strange. They walked together like a pair of security guards, moving along the perimeter of the fence, occasionally pausing to check something underneath, sniffing then moving on. When they finished the entire fence they would go into the tool shed for a few minutes, come back out and repeat.

My daughter wouldn't give me the secret to how she was training them, just that she was.

"We're headed out again, Lev," I said. "Today and tomorrow, then we quit."

"I know you want to find them, Nila, and I know why."

"I'm concerned about the child."

"And?"

"Her mother."

"Nila, we both know better, you want your father's rifle back."

"That, too."

I paused to think if Lev really was still alive, how he would have probably stopped her from leaving in the first place. Katie was the only one who said it, but I know they blamed me and my attitude toward Meg for her leaving. Lev in his often righteous stance would have made me apologize.

One thing was right, I did want my father's rifle back.

I bent down to pull a couple weeds from Lev's grave. "Why do you always get the most weeds?"

"Because you notice them more."

"Not true."

"Look at your stepmother's grave. It is overgrown. I hate to think how the grave of someone you truly did not like would look."

I glanced over to Lisa's grave. Sure enough there were more weeds than at anyone else's. Tossing down what I yanked from Lev's grave, I went to Lisa's and crouched down. "Sorry, Lisa." I grabbed some weeds and when I did, Sean stood off in the distance waving.

I returned the wave, tossed the weeds aside, and stood. "I'll get those later." And then walked over to Sean. "I guess we're ready to do our meet?"

"Yeah, just waiting on you. I figured you were out here… you know…"

"Praying?" I asked.

"Yeah, anything interesting?"

"Just in my conversation with Lev, he told me he thinks I'm only searching for Meg to get back my father's rifle."

"I have news for you," Sean said. "We all think that."

That made me smile as I returned to the cabin with him.

The map was spread open on the kitchen table and only Fleck and Ben stood there. Bella had the kids at the RV.

"I packed you a lunch today," said Ben when I approached. "Since you were gone yesterday four hours."

"Hey," Fleck said. "Why didn't you pack a lunch yesterday when I took her?"

"I didn't think you would be gone that long, you only went to check Lyndora," Ben replied.

"They had that big old spooky hotel," Fleck said. "We had to check that out. But…" He turned and looked back at Sean. "Your turn today."

"Do we need anything?" Sean asked. "That we can look for?"

"Hand soap," Fleck answered. "We can never have enough hand soap."

That made me roll my eyes and shake my head. We picked up hand soap every trip. "Okay, so any idea where we're going?"

"Well, we checked Lyndora," Ben answered. "And all Butler areas. You could check them again or go out further. You haven't been to West Liberty."

I replied, "We have traveled Route Eight, and Four-Twenty-Two extensively."

"You said," Sean interjected, "she was calling out on the radio. Did she pick up any areas, maybe?"

I shook my head. "Katie said no."

"Did she take the radio?" Sean asked.

Suddenly, I felt the color drain from my face. I hadn't even thought about it because we just never used it. "I don't know."

"No one checked?" Sean questioned.

"I took it from her and put it in the sewing room closet," I said.

Fleck left the table. "I'll go check."

"It's on the bottom," I told him.

A few seconds after he walked away, Fleck returned. "It's gone. She took it I guess. Why we didn't think about it, I don't know."

"You need that back as well as the rifle," Sean said. "You don't want her calling out and giving your location."

I shook my head. "Why didn't we think about that? Pisses me off. Nine days and we're just thinking about it now."

Ben replied, "Because we don't use the radio. I'm curious, Sean, what made you think of it today?"

"I was trying to figure out where my socks went and…"

Sean noticed I pointed at Fleck.

"You took my socks?" Sean asked. "Why would you take my socks?"

"Thought they were mine." Fleck lifted his hands.

"Yeah," Ben said. "You have to hang your socks somewhere he doesn't see. He takes everyone's socks."

"I don't get why," Sean said. "You're out there all the time, grab a pack."

"I don't think about it until I need them," Fleck replied. "Anyhow, get to the point. You were looking for socks…"

"And I saw my radio and that's when it hit me," Sean answered.

"You have a radio?" I asked.

"Yeah, short distance, handheld, I took it from The Colony. I turned it off and took the batteries out before I got anywhere near Butler. I was monitoring and it had been a day since I heard anything."

"There was chatter?" Ben questioned.

"Yeah, not much though. Camps, I think, not sure," Sean said. "So I thought if she had the radio and she called out, maybe got a response. Maybe that's where she was headed."

Fleck snapped his finger. "She did get that one response. She probably tried calling out again."

I asked Sean, "Do you remember any names or places?"

111

"Um…" He tilted his head. "Let me think." He closed his eyes. "Sister something, Somerset."

I nodded. "That's a possibility. That's southeast. There are survivors there? That's really good to know."

"One more," Sean said. "Brady? Does that sound familiar."

"East Brady maybe?" I suggested.

"I couldn't tell you." Sean lifted his hands.

I glanced down to the map and put my finger on it. "East Brady. Twenty miles east. On the Allegheny River, really small. They could perimeter off that whole town easily. I can see that being a survival town."

"Then that's where we go," Sean said.

"Wait," Fleck stated. "I don't know. We've run into some bad people since this whole thing started. I don't know that it's safe just driving up to a small town. They may shoot you. I would."

"Oh stop," I scoffed. "No, you wouldn't. You'd ask questions first."

Ben asked, "Sean, does your radio work?"

"It should. I took the batteries out."

"Why don't you do this," Ben suggested. "Take the radio, call out to East Brady when you start to get close. Let them know you're coming."

"Uh…" Sean seemed in debate. "I don't know. Listening sure, but calling out. I don't know. To be honest, I don't want The Colony to hear my voice, and we can't have Nila call out on the same chance."

"You said they were short range," Fleck said. "What is the range?"

"Fifty miles," Sean replied.

"Do you think The Colony might be within fifty miles?"

"I couldn't begin to tell you. I don't want to know, and I really don't want to take the chance. Not after the helicopter and you guys saying you saw that convoy."

"He's got a point," I said. "Okay, we take it, we only monitor. We take Sean's old Dodge; it will come across a lot less threatening than a truck. Chances are they're going to have guards on post more for the dead. I really believe if it's the people of East Brady, they'll stop us before they shoot us."

Ben glanced at me. "Do you want to take that chance?"

"I have to, I really do." I paused then smiled. "I want my father's rifle back."

"Oh, wow." I showed Sean a half sandwich as we drove. "So good. Want some?"

"No, I'm fine."

"I can't believe Ben made this bread. It is really good. Are you sure?'

"Positive, you should have had breakfast."

"Nah, I'm not really a breakfast eater." I picked at the peanut butter.

"That was an hour ago."

"I got really hungry."

"I see that."

I unscrewed the cap on the Scooby Doo thermos and took a swig, cringing slightly. Even though I knew it was in there, the taste of powdered milk always threw me off at first. "I miss real milk."

"Ben packed you a thermos of milk?" he asked.

"It goes with peanut butter."

"I would have thought coffee."

"Nah, he's limiting my intake."

Sean laughed. "Why?"

"Why? I don't know. He said he needed to, and since he's the doctor I agreed."

"You think it's stress."

"Again, I don't know. I mean…who would question Ben?"

"Me," Sean said. "If he walked up and took coffee from me and said he was limiting my intake, I'd ask why."

"I guess we're different."

"I guess, I mean, I really don't know you that well, you just never struck me as the type that would accept something without asking."

"I wouldn't have a while ago." I took another bite. "A lot has changed recently."

"Well, have you changed some since I met you?"

I watched him look down to the radio on the seat and lift it as if it would make something come through.

"Want me to try to call out? I'll do my best Pitts-burghese."

"What the heck is Pittsburghese?" he asked.

"Just the local dialect."

"No, we'll just leave it on and stay radio silent. It's not far." He set the radio back down on the seat.

He was right. Shortly after I finished my half sandwich, we saw the East Brady One Mile sign. But as we came up on it, we didn't see any movement.

There was a huge fence erected and several cars parked outside it as a blockade, but we didn't see anyone.

Until we drove closer.

It looked like there were people on the ground by the fence, a couple flopped over on the hood of a car.

"Deaders?" I asked.

"Let's see." Sean placed the car in park about forty feet from the blockade. He reached into the back seat for a backpack, lifted it to his lap and reached inside.

He pulled out a pair of binoculars, then opened the door.

I stepped out when Sean walked in front of the hood, raising the binoculars and adjusting them.

"Take a look." He handed them to me.

I was never really good with looking through them, and it took me a few seconds to find something recognizable. I was only getting trees and car roofs. Then I scanned down and saw the body of a man resting chest first on the hood.

From what I could see he didn't look like a deader, nor were his clothes tattered and blood soaked, but he had a bullet hole in his head. "Might be infected."

"Might be."

"Or it could have been the work of The Colony."

"That, too."

"Stay back and cover me, I'm gonna go look." I handed him the binoculars.

"Why are you going to look?"

"In case they're infected. I'm immune."

"Yep, well, me too. Not to the bites but to the virus. So let's go."

I already had my gun, but Sean went back and retrieved a rifle from the car and together we walked to the barricade.

There were several bodies. Only one woman. All of them were armed, two were dead with their backs against the fence, the remainder just lay where they were shot.

As soon as I was close enough I could see the telltale marks of the virus. "They hadn't turned," I said. "They look like late stage, but not turning."

"So it's definitely the work of The Colony. They would do this," Sean said.

"Looks like it, but…" I moved closer. "They are all around the same stage."

"How can you tell?"

"The veins on the neck and jaw. Usually the black veins are all over the face when they turn. None of these people have those."

"We need to be careful," Sean said. "There could be ragers around."

"I don't think so. These people were definitely put down. But doesn't it seem weird to you that they're all armed, and they were all on guard duty with all of them infected?" Another step and another closer look.

A male voice called out from the distance. "I wouldn't get too close or touch them if I were you."

I glanced up.

An older man, maybe in his late sixties, approached the fence.

"They might still be contagious," he said.

"I'm immune," I replied.

"How do you know that?"

Sean answered, "There are government run survivor areas, they test. Probably the same people who came through and killed these people."

The man at the gate shook his head. "No one did that but them. That big guy over there." He pointed, then hesitantly asked, "You from one of those survivor areas?"

I shook my head. "No. At least not anymore." Then tuned to look at where he'd pointed. I hadn't seen the man, he was on the other side of a truck, seated on the ground. His was slumped with his back against the truck, shotgun between his legs and his head partially blown off.

"They all knew they were sick," the man said. "How could they not. A lot of our camp got sick."

"How many were there?" I asked.

"We had sixty survivors here from all over. Now … twelve. Several took off. We have healthy inside. I can't let you in. For you and for us."

I lifted my hand. "I completely understand."

"We're actually looking for someone," Sean said. "A woman. She was part of our camp and she would have come here not long ago. Has a daughter, driving a station wagon."

"Oh, yes, her. Yes. She left. She and the kid were two of the ones that left."

"Do you know if she was sick?" I asked.

"I thought most of them that left were, but she said she wasn't."

Hurriedly, I racked my brain trying to remember if Meg was a blue bracelet like me and was immune, or was a yellow like Lev. I couldn't recall. "Do you know how long ago she left?" I questioned further.

"Two days. She wasn't here long."

"Thank you," Sean said. "You've been very helpful."

"You're welcome. Good luck."

"Same to you," I replied as we turned.

"I'd tell ya…" the man called out. "I'd say I hope you find her, but…for the sake of your camp, I hope you don't."

We returned to the car and got inside.

Sean started the engine and turned to me with his hand still on the ignition. "Well? What do you think?"

"I think he was being honest. I feel bad for him. So many people dead. This virus scares me more now than it did when it started."

"Me too. What about Meg?"

"We found her…sort of," I said. "I think knowing that she's been here, I think it's time we stop looking."

"I couldn't agree more. Back to the cabin?"

"No. Let's get Fleck his damn hand soap and socks, then we'll head back."

"Sounds good. And…and I think I'll take that peanut butter sandwich now."

"After seeing that?" I asked.

"I'm hungry."

"And they call me strange." I reached down for the lunch bag Ben had packed and pulled out the half sandwich for Sean as he backed up and turned the car around.

I felt at peace for searching and even a bit resolved, my father's rifle or not. We could put it behind us, put the Meg situation and mystery to rest. Now we just needed to get hand soap and socks and head back to the cabin for normalcy.

Fleck's obsession with hand soap baffled me. It didn't matter what kind, it could be strawberry scented and he still wanted it. I wasn't sure how long he had it, but I noticed the obscene amount of bottles he had right after Lev had passed away. Apparently he had been grabbing a bottle or two whenever we went out. He even had soap from The Colony.

It would be different if he was using it up fast, but he wasn't. He was just collecting it. I asked him why and he said when things were going bad during the outbreak, he couldn't find hand soap.

I didn't recall that shortage, or any shortage at all.

Then again, when things finally crashed, we were at the cabin.

Sean and I stopped and at the first store they had plenty. Maybe in Florida lack of hand soap was a thing, but it looked to be plentiful in Pennsylvania.

I grabbed him eight bottles in hopes he wouldn't ask for more for a while. I didn't know where he was going to put it.

We talked on the short drive about what the reactions of the others would be to the news of not only finding Meg but of the outbreak in East Brady.

As we pulled up the road to the cabin, I found it odd that I could hear Caesar barking as we neared the top.

My heart raced and chest pounded as I thought, Not again, please don't let the deaders have gotten in.

But just before the top of the road, parked on the crest, was Ben's station wagon.

"Shit." Sean shoved the gear in park. "Meg."

I pulled out my pistol and opened the door. I saw Meg standing at the fence facing Ben.

"Don't let her in, Ben," I shouted, gun extended. "Do not open that gate." I ran past the station wagon, and toward them. "She may be infected."

That was when I saw Three Sixteen was trying to push Ben back.

Had Meg turned? She wasn't charging the fence like the infected did.

Slowly she turned around, she was crying. "I'm sorry," she sobbed. "I'm so sorry."

She didn't look sick, not from where I stood. "Let me see your neck."

"What?" she asked, confused.

"Let me see your neck."

Meg lifted her chin.

"Lower the collar on your tee shirt," I told her. "Let me see."

Fingers gripping the collar, she lowered it some. She didn't need to lower it much and I saw the start of the dark veins.

"Son of a bitch," I barked. "You brought it here?"

"Please. No. Listen." She held up her hands. "I don't care what you do to me. I don't care. But help Maura. Please help my baby."

"Where is she?" I asked.

"In the car." She broke down again. I lowered my gun, turned, and walked back to the station wagon.

Sean stood behind me.

Whispering, I asked him, "Did you see her in the car?"

"I didn't look."

Giving him a slight nod, I walked by him to the wagon. I first peeked in the windshield but didn't see Maura in the front. Then I moved to the back and looked in the windows.

The little girl was covered with a blanket. She lay on her side, her head resting on her arm as a pillow.

My first thought was what the hell was the matter with Meg? It was eighty degrees and not only didn't she leave her sick child in the car, she covered her in a blanket and, dangerously, she left the windows all up.

Immediately, I grabbed the handle. I wanted to get fresh air in the car for Maura, but when I opened the back door, fresh air wasn't going to matter.

It blasted me, like a bomb, with the smell of death.

Sour, pungent, and rotten, my eyes cast to Maura. The blanket had come onto to her shoulders, but what flesh was exposed was thick and swollen and discolored. I didn't stand there long enough to see if she had been infected or turned or even how she died.

My stomach flopped and the contents of my belly make their way up my esophagus.

I spun from the car and barely made it a foot before I threw up.

It was a combination of everything about that moment, the surprise of Meg, fear that the deaders had invaded camp, all topped off with the sight of that little girl in the back of the car.

When I finished, I glanced up. Meg still stood there by the fence, watching me, crying.

I stood straight. I wanted to scream at her, shout, You left this cabin to find safety and that killed your daughter.

But I couldn't.

That pain in her face wasn't her illness, it was her heart-ache. A pain I too had felt. She didn't even realize her child had died.

I couldn't help but feel sorry for her, hurt for her. I didn't know how I could help her, if I could even help her at all.

I would think of something.

FOURTEEN

BEING HUMAN

Sean
July 30

Nila had a really strange routine of getting up in the morning, walking the property and talking to herself. Actually, she said she talked to Lev. Now I knew she was well aware she wasn't speaking to his ghost. She was working through her grief, missing him and finding her own way to deal with it.

It bred comments from the others—Fleck stating he thought it was harmful, Ben was keeping an eye out. Me, if she really truly believed she was talking to actual Lev, I'd worry some. But the answers she got from 'Lev' were from her years of time with him, her memories of what he would say.

At least that was my take.

Of course, my take was also the cabin was good for Nila. When I had last seen her at The Colony, sure she was healthy, but at the cabin, she looked good, relaxed, had even gained some weight.

But from the moment she decided she couldn't let Meg die outside the fence, I saw it weighing down on her.

She claimed it was because the infected moved on memory before they died and became deaders, that somehow

122

Meg would unlock the gate if she turned out there. Instead, Nila said to allow Meg to comfortably move to the brink of death and then help her cross before she turned.

Personally, I didn't buy her reasoning. I think the human being in her was coming out despite the tough act she put on.

She had a little tent and she set it up for Meg far from the cabin. It was so hot out, but Meg was fevered and didn't know.

Only Nila and I tended to her and checked on her. With the exception of Katie, the others were susceptible to the virus. Ben argued that he was a doctor and he didn't get it from Lev.

From what I had seen, the virus was mutating and changing fast. There was the possibility that how it was today was not how it would act tomorrow.

Same virus, different actions.

I was told when I was at The Colony that had the current strain been the one loose during the original outbreak, none of us would have survived.

The infected would have turned too fast and there would have been too many of them.

We had discussed the same thing over dinner the previous evening in the cabin, then we talked about the virus.

It was reminiscent of the outbreak days, early on when it was all everyone could think or talk about. I bounced between focusing on June and on the conversation at the table.

I wish I was as ignorant to everything as children were.

In actuality, June and the baby, Christian, were the only ones ignorant about it.

Sawyer and Katie knew it well.

Katie was depressed about it some. Her usually cheerful and bubbly self kept asking, "What happens if they don't fix the new virus? Will everyone die?"

The grown-up response of, "Don't worry about it, it will be fine," wasn't sitting with her. Of course not, everyone was too focused about it.

I knew it mutated and was out there, but finding June, being at the cabin, had me in the mindset we had escaped it. We were fine. As long as some bird or animal didn't drop it on us, we would prevail.

Even I, immune as I was, worried about it constantly because Meg was on the property.

It didn't surprise me that Fleck and Bella were slightly angry with Nila about allowing Meg on the property, and I saw their point.

The decision was made. Whether it was like Nila said, to prevent her turning on the other side of the fence, or Nila being human and giving Meg some dignity to die with care and comfort.

I didn't see her lasting much longer. Meg's grief was deep. It was grief and guilt. A lethal combination I too had felt.

But for all the negatives to her being on the property, we were learning this new phase of the virus. Ben and Nila both said it was different than with Lev.

Meg coughed more, her fever was high, she complained her entire body not only hurt but burned, and her eyes…her eyes were quickly losing color.

We were our own scientific study group.

It took a while to get June down for the night. Even though Christian was younger, he was almost the same size and she just wanted to play with the 'baby.' Ben was reading and still awake, so I asked him to keep an ear out for her while I walked the property perimeter.

I didn't need to. Not with the dynamic duo of Three Sixteen and Caesar. I couldn't figure out how they learned so much so fast. As much as everyone praised the little girl, I believed their zombie skills were honed in long before they joined the group at the cabin. But I didn't see the dogs, and they weren't in the cabin.

I started to get concerned, almost ready to call out for them when Fleck and Nila's attempt at having a conversation at a whisper failed.

I followed the sound of their voices as they carried in the night. Their talk about how much they missed McDonald's and other take-out foods led me to the RV. I didn't see them, but I did find Caesar and Three Sixteen. Both dogs were seated ten feet from Meg's tent, while Fleck and Nila were on the roof of the RV.

Hoping they didn't mind, I climbed up the side ladder, announcing my arrival as I did.

"Hey, my man," Fleck said. "Beer?" He extended out a bottle.

"Thanks." I took it. It felt cold in my hand. "Nice." After twisting the cap I chugged a few good drinks. "Nothing like a cold beer on a hot night."

"Tell me about it," Fleck replied.

It didn't take me long to figure out why they were up there. Nila had her rifle. Not only was there a silencer on it, but night vision as she watched Meg's tent.

"She that close?" I asked, taking a seat on the roof.

"She's close," Nila answered. "Not close enough for Ben's comfort to euthanize. Although, in my opinion, she's ready emotionally."

"So why aren't we?" Fleck asked.

"Ben said as a doctor, he has to try. He's trying." Nila shrugged. "Call it a hunch, but she's gonna turn. I'm not taking a chance of her turning in the middle of the night. She'll be infected and they move on memory. They can open doors with ease. I'll be on edge until she turns or passes."

"Maybe someone should be on her all the time," I suggested.

Nila nodded. "I'm taking night shift tonight. Fleck will take tomorrow."

"I'll take a shift," I told her.

Fleck nudged Nila. "I don't think we're going to need that."

I knew the infected and deaders as well as anyone, and I didn't know what Fleck meant until I saw the dogs suddenly stand at attention, necks extended toward the tent.

The tent was dark and there was no noise. But the reaction of the dogs was enough for Nila to stand, extend her rifle, and take aim.

We watched those dogs. They were frozen for the longest time. There was no conversation on the roof of the RV; we held our breath.

I chalked it up to a false alarm, until Caser barked. He barked once then again.

The small tent rippled some as if caught by the wind. Caesar darted at the tent in and out, but didn't go in. His barking increased when the entrance flap moved violently, almost as if Meg struggled.

"Ha," Fleck said softly. "So much for opening a door with ease."

Nila muttered a "Yeah" entirely focused and watching.

Then with a whip of the flap, Caesar barking insanely, Meg charged out.

One shot. One fast silent 'whiff' of the rifle and Meg went down.

Man, Nila was good.

She stood staring out for a few seconds after lowering her weapon. Almost waiting to see if Meg moved but she didn't.

Nila had done her job.

She turned around and faced me. "Now we can sleep and get back to normal."

"What um…about the body?" I asked.

"Let's you and I move her into the tent tonight and we'll deal with it in the morning."

"Oh, man," Fleck gloated. "This is one of the times I am glad I'm not immune."

I looked at Nila, who kept staring out to Meg. There was a bit of relief on Nila's face. In the week and a half that I had been there we had done nothing but look for Meg. Not to mention my arrival was greeted with deaders on the property.

Nila said that since Meg was down we could get back to normal. Apparently, I hadn't experienced 'normal.' At the cabin, I truly looked forward to it.

FIFTEEN

WIDENING APPROACH

Nila
September 20

The cold evening weather arrived quickly, but thankfully the days were still warm enough that the house kept the heat high enough inside so we didn't have to use firewood. The firewood thing made me miss Lev. No one could chop it as efficiently and as fast as he had.

Fleck and Sean tried. I didn't nag them, though I wanted to.

Lev had been gone almost three months and it was still hard to believe. My body believed it. With my two daughters, I never did show like I was pregnant. The cooler weather afforded me the chance to wear bigger clothes and cover up, because I still wasn't ready to let anyone know.

It had been calm and peaceful.

We had a few infected since Meg had died, most deaders would come to the fence. The infected and how fast they moved added some excitement. Hearing the dogs bark, watching Three Sixteen nudge the kids back, getting the infected before it climbed the fence.

Trips for supplies were geared toward stocking up rather than need. We ended up with some pretty great tomatoes.

Thank God Ben knew how to can them because I would have just cut them and tossed them in the jars. So many tomatoes and very few jars.

We did replenish the chicken coop—Fleck and Sean came back with some chickens. He found them walking the road like I used to see ducks doing.

I didn't want to ask how they caught them.

It was awesome to get eggs, but we were getting them faster than we could eat them. Who knew three chickens could pop out so many.

I asked Ben to pickle them and he looked at me as if I were nuts. What was so wrong with pickled eggs?

Other than an occasional desire for odd food, my behavior hadn't changed.

Though I broke my own rule.

The people in East Brady were on my mind a lot. So much so I pulled out the radio.

I checked and double-checked with Sean if The Colony had the ability to hone in on a radio. He told me if it could be done, they were doing it. They were scanning frequencies for chatter. He did tell me if the signal was clear, common sense would tell The Colony they were close.

It wasn't The Colony's policy to just grab people for the town, they invited them, like they did with Cobb County.

However, in my case, we were fearful about them wanting Katie.

East Brady was a possible and viable trading post for us. So, against everything I said I would do, I reached out to them. Of course, I communicated using my best Pittsburgh accent.

Anyone in the Pittsburgh area would say they didn't talk like that, I swore I didn't talk like that. The dialect had to be really bad for another Pittsburgher to say, "Hey you really sound Pittsburgh."

Local comedians racked up video views by poking fun of our dialect.

Most of us were guilty of it when we didn't think we were. Using wrong vowel sounds, making two syllable words into one. Like 'fire' was 'fy' and 'shower' was 'shire.'

Things like that.

Add a bit of a tang and make it drastic and you sounded like the comedic acts, and that was exactly what I did.

Plus, I tossed in the very funky 'yinz' word.

"Remember in history books," I said on the radio. "How Pittsburgh because of the rivers was a great trade area? Maybe East Brady can be. Huck?" I asked the man I had met at the gate the one day.

"If more people come out of hiding sure."

"How you holding up for the cold?"

"We're getting there. You?"

"We're getting there. Biff and Skip are trying," I said, using my code names for Fleck and Sean.

"But they're no Von," Huck said, meaning Lev.

"No, they are no Von. Well, gonna end this for this morning. Let me know if you need anything."

"Sounds good. But Spice Girl."

"Yes."

"I have to ask. Not sure where you are, but…did they come there yet?"

"Who?" I asked.

"The people. We got a late afternoon visit yesterday, they drove up to the gate in a black SUV and jeep. Some people called The Colony."

Hearing that made my heart stop.

"I never heard of them," said Huck. "So I guess you didn't either."

I knew that was a lie, and Huck was covering in case they were listening.

"No, I haven't," I said. "Who are they?"

"Government and military I guess. They seemed nice. They are looking for people to fill their cities. I respectfully declined. Especially after the virus hit us."

"I don't blame you."

"I wanted to give you the heads-up in case they happen upon you. They're searching for survivors."

"I appreciate that, Huck, I do. Talk to you in a couple days."

"Keep me posted."

I set down the microphone and turned off the radio. Huck was giving us a warning. He knew I had been with The Colony at some point; it was one of the first things I told him when we met at his fence.

We never discussed it in detail.

Maybe he thought I was running from them. Either way, Huck in his own words gave us the clear sign to stay away and be ready.

The sound of Ben clearing his throat drew my attention and I turned to face him.

"I heard," Ben said.

"Honestly, I am not making the same mistakes I made last year."

131

"I know," Ben replied. "Plus, you already met them."

"Do you think I'm responsible?" I asked. "I mean, Sean said they listen for chatter. I called out for Brady."

"Maybe. But they didn't attack the town, they didn't shoot anyone. The ones that remain must be immune."

"I hope."

"What do you think?" Ben asked.

"I think we need to keep an eye out. Have a plan for hiding me and Katie. A story we can all stick to in case they do show up. We're really buried in the trees."

"Not for long," Ben said.

"What do you mean?"

"The leaves are falling. We'll be more easily spotted and eventually we're going to have to light a fire for warmth. Smoke rises."

"Then we'll have to be diligent. You don't think they'll be forceful, do you?"

"They weren't with East Brady," Ben said. "However, Katie isn't there."

"Do they really need her that bad?"

Ben shrugged. "I'd say they tested all they could with her, if they do need her it's to go forward."

I stared down to my hands.

"You're not thinking of moving, are you?" Ben asked.

"No, absolutely not. This is my home. I'm standing my ground."

"If they are looking for us, they'll find us, you know."

"I do." I nodded and jumped in my seat when Fleck flew into the room.

"There you are. Thank God. We have a problem," Fleck said hurriedly.

Seeing the look on his face, the panic, immediately made me think The Colony had showed up.

"What is it?" I asked.

"Your daughter," Fleck replied.

"Honestly, Fleck, it's getting a little ridiculous you fighting with a five-year-old…" I sniffed. "What is that smell? Oh, it's horrible, is that you? Ben needs to talk to you about your diet because…"

Thump.

Fleck wasted no time, had no tact, and probably enjoyed tossing the source of the smell my way. It landed hard on the desk in front of the radio, causing me to push away and jump from my chair when I saw what it was. A human hand.

"What the hell?" I asked, shocked.

"Your daughter"—Fleck pointed to the hand—"was playing with it."

It was hard to believe at first; he was talking about a five-year-old. How was she playing with a decomposed hand? The next question that came to my mind was why, the last was, where did it come from?

After freaking on Fleck to get the hand out of the house, I walked from the office with Ben, my mind spinning as I sought out Katie.

"Is she mentally ill?" I asked Ben. "This is a serious question. I mean, do I have a Michael Myers in the making?"

"She's not going to slaughter us in our sleep," he replied. "You need to remember this is her world now. These kids are growing up with dead bodies walking up and trying to eat them. A new normal you and I still can't adjust to. It doesn't scare her."

"It has to, and it should for her own safety. I still get terrified."

"Me too. But before we jump to conclusions let's talk to Katie."

We didn't have to seek her out. Katie was sat on the top step of the porch, her hands tapping on her knees with an okay, you got me look.

She didn't deny it. Not one bit when I asked her if she had that hand.

"So you were playing with it?" I asked.

"Who told you that?"

"Fleck."

"That is not true. I was not playing with it."

"Oh my God," Fleck barked. "She lies with a perfectly straight face."

"I'm not lying," Katie defended.

"Katie." Fleck tried to be reasonable and I could tell it was a chore. "You were chasing Caesar yelling 'give me back my hand,' and when you got it, you put it on the ground and teased Three Sixteen with it."

"That's not playing," she said.

"What is it?" Fleck asked.

"Training."

"You're training the dogs with a deader hand?" Fleck quizzed.

"And other parts."

I didn't mean to, but I screamed. A short scream of shock. "Katie, what other parts?"

"Just parts. Some I don't know what they are. One is part of a head."

Again, I screamed. "Oh my, Katie, you've been playing with body parts?"

"Training Mommy. I want the dogs to be zombie protectors."

"That already are," Fleck said.

"Three Sixteen came here trained," Katie said. "I trained Caesar."

"Where did you get the body parts?" I asked.

"Caesar," she replied. "He digs them up all the time."

Immediately I panicked and wanted to run to the little cemetery,

"Where?"

"Outside the fence facing the hill. He dug a hole there and climbs under and gets parts. He likes them. The zombie parts," she said. "When he brought the first one and I took it off of him he barked and barked and sniffed it out. So I hide them so he can sniff and find them. But today he took off with one. Fleck got it before I did."

"He's not…" I said. "Caesar is not digging them up in our cemetery, is he?"

"No." Katie shook her head. "Besides, he only likes the infected body parts."

I closed my eyes and turned to Ben. "I'm not even going to ask how she knows that."

"I will," Ben said. "Katie how can you know that?"

"Because one day he went out and came back with a foot. It wasn't a deader foot. It didn't have the black lines. He dropped it and went back out and came back with a real deader part, then got mad and barked when I wanted it."

"Okay two…" Ben held up two fingers. "Two questions beg an answer. First, where do you put the body parts you train with?"

Katie bit her lip. "I cover them with the stuff we use in the outhouse."

"And," Ben continued, "I don't know if Katie can answer this one, but why is Caesar even able to find body parts outside the fence? I thought when we took them out, we moved the bodies to a pit a mile or so from here."

Fleck raised his hand. "Guilty. I…I dug some shallow graves, I thought if I made a perimeter of dead, it might keep the dead away."

"Not working," I said.

"Well, in my defense we don't get any coming to that section of the fence anymore," Fleck replied.

"Okay, true, that—" The sound of a helicopter in the distance drew my attention. I stepped back away from the porch and looked up to the sky. Whether it was or not, it looked like it was moving our way. "Ben, kids inside now." I rushed forward, grabbed Katie, and took her into the Cabin. "Stay here, do not leave."

"Are they coming for me, Mommy?"

"I hope not. Just stay put." I ran down the hall to the closet, grabbing for my father's best rifle and ammo. I heard the others all enter the cabin, immediately discussing whether to shutter the place.

"Where's your mom?" I heard Ben ask.

"Getting a gun," said Katie.

It was just about loaded when Ben called for me. "Nila, what are you doing?"

I glanced up from my rifle, Fleck and Sean stood in the hall as well.

"Defending my home," I replied.

"You need to hide, you and Katie," Ben stated.

"No, I need to fight this."

Fleck questioned, "What? You're gonna go out there and shoot at a chopper?"

"If I have to."

"Okay, I'm in," Fleck said.

I smiled and widened the closet door. "Take your pick."

"Just don't grab mine," added Sean as he walked by me to the closet. "I'm in."

At that point the chopper was loud, too loud. I knew it was upon us.

"Nila," Ben begged as he followed me to the door. "This is insane. If they don't come guns blazing, they will if you go out there and shoot. Don't...do this."

I held firm to the door handle. "This is my home, Ben. They're here for my daughter and you know it. I won't give up my child without a fight."

"We don't know this," Ben said. "They may only want to talk."

"With a chopper?" I asked. "You heard. Huck said they drove to his gate. Nah." I shook my head. "They aren't here for a chat. You know that and even said it yourself."

"Nila, please," Ben said. "Just stay inside."

"Wait for them to bust the door down? No, Ben, if they wanted a peaceful entrance they wouldn't have come in so loud. I'm sorry. Get the kids in the floor." I opened the door.

It was even louder than I expected when we stepped on to the porch. I could feel the force of the blades whipping, lifting the dirt off the yard.

What the hell were they doing?

I stepped down the first step and I saw there wasn't just one helicopter but two, hovering low. Ropes dangled from the open side door, each lowering an armed colony soldier.

"Oh, fuck this." I raised my rifle, got the leg of the soldier in my scope, and as quick as I was, before I could pop off a shot, I felt it hit my right arm. Instantly, my arm went numb and a shift of my eyes to my bicep allowed me to see the tiny silver dart. As if I were having a stroke, I lost control of my right arm and the rifle toppled, no matter how hard I tried to hold on to it.

I was able to reach with my left hand and pull the dart, but by the time I removed it from my skin, my eyes went blurry.

"Nila." Sean stepped in front of me. "Get in the…" His words slowed down, and voice deepened. "Cab…in."

There were two or three Seans and every movement of his head caused trails of color streaks.

Was I teetering?

I was still aware enough to see Fleck go down.

My lips felt swollen, I tried to speak.

Sean grabbed my arms, his fingers felt like daggers, the slightest pressure caused pain. Pain I knew was there but in a way I couldn't truly experience it.

The dream-like state grew deeper.

"Nila," Sean said. With a jolt of his body he leaned into me then, just like Fleck dropped.

I tried to move, I really did, but I only fell to my knees.

It was a military invasion on my land. There wasn't enough space to lower the choppers so they dropped the men right into my yard. They rushed by me into the cabin and there was nothing I could do about it. I was helpless to even stay awake, let alone move.

Before I could even register anything, I saw the grass and a portion of Sean's leg. Closer, closer, and then, helicopter noise blasting, enough wind coming at me to take my breath away, along with shouting voices, all faded…I was out.

Quiet.

Extreme quiet accompanied by a daggering and pounding headache. I could feel the blades of grass against my cheek and my eyelashes as I fluttered my eyes.

I knew instantly I had been drugged. I remembered that. There was no question, but when I fully opened my eyes, I saw a leg. And when I lifted my head, I was shocked to see I was still at the cabin.

Somehow, some part of me expected to be taken. They had done such a huge, dramatic invasion of my little bit of land.

When that reality struck me I sprang up.

Along with a headache, my mouth was dry and my legs weak. But not so weak I couldn't pull myself together.

As soon as I stood I saw Sean lying near me and Fleck a few feet away. Both still had their weapons near them. Three Sixteen was on her side, too. Motionless.

Were they dead? Or were they, like me, drugged.

"Sean," I called out. "Fleck?"

Neither of them responded. I didn't see any blood, but my concern was elsewhere.

Fearful, I hurried up the steps. The front door was open and I raced inside.

Ben was on the floor behind the couch and near him was Caesar. Like Sean and Fleck they didn't move. Ben lay on his side and I was able to see a larger dart than the one that hit me was in his neck.

"No, no, no," I screamed out. "Katie!"

"Nila!" I heard the muffled call of my name, then I heard the sound of the babies crying. "Nila! Down here!"

The heaviness in my chest lifted and I felt somewhat relieved.

I hurried to the center of the room. The throw rug on the hatch was disturbed and shifted. I reached down lifting the hatch.

When I did, the cries were louder. Bella held both June and Christian, crouched down tight in that crawl space storage with Sawyer next to her.

One child was not there.

Katie.

My daughter…was gone.

SIXTEEN

TOO MANY HOLES

Sean

Whatever drug they used on me, Fleck, and Ben was different than the one they used on Nila. Hers was smaller, almost like a woman version. It didn't make sense. They targeted the cabin and had made special darts for each person.

It made me leery on what was in there.

Clearly, Nila woke before us.

When I came to she was screaming. Calling out, "Katie!" over and over while both dogs barked.

"Nila," Bella shouted. "Stop. Please."

"I have to find my daughter."

Before I opened my eyes fully, I squeezed them. When I did the headache worsened and I sat up, and then stumbled to a stand.

Fleck was on his back. He groaned and moved some.

"Fleck." I nudged him with my foot. "Fleck, get up."

Once steady on my feet I felt the pinch to the base of my neck where it met my shoulder, that was when I discovered the dart. The larger needle still embedded in my skin.

I pulled it out.

My wits slowly returned and I watched Bella chase Nila toward the gate.

I tried to move. "Nila," I called out.

Nila stopped and ran to me. "Sean," she said. "She's gone. Katie isn't here. I have to find her."

Bella approached. "She's not on the property, Nila. You're confused. Listen to me. She's not here," Bella said. "I know. They took her from my arms."

Nila was physically unstable and I could see that. Her color was off and whatever drug they pumped into us was still pulsing in her veins.

"Nila." Ben followed her back into the cabin. "Please, calm down."

"Let me help you." I reached out. "You're swaying."

"I'm fine," she snapped.

"All of us!" Ben lifted his voice. "We need to get hydrated. It's important."

"We need to get my daughter,"

"I agree," Ben said. "But do we know where? Did Huck mention anything about where they were?"

"If he didn't," Fleck added, "we ride to East Brady. Don't use the radio and get him to reach out to them. You think he will?"

"Yeah, if I tell them they took Katie. He will. I'm sure."

"Then that's step one." Fleck then faced me. "Sean, you were with them. Can you go back? Maybe say you changed your mind."

"I can," I replied. "I can reach out to them. Use my radio. I don't think they're very far."

Ben shook his head. "That would be suspicious. They storm our camp, take Katie, and then you call. They're gonna know something is up."

"I know this," I said. "I know they can be brutal with infected. They want to eliminate the virus. That is their number one goal. If they can't cure it, they will eradicate it. They want to cure it. They don't want the human race to die."

"They have a funny way of showing it," Fleck said. "Shooting up towns."

"I am not defending that." I lifted my hand. "I'm just saying this is their way to get rid of it. They didn't shoot any of us. They knocked us out. The fact that they came in on choppers tells me they wanted Katie fast. Maybe they're on the brink of a cure."

"They could have asked," Ben said.

Nila shook her head. "It wouldn't have made a difference. I wouldn't have responded and I wouldn't have given up my daughter to be an experiment."

"And that," I stated, "is why they did what they did. They took her. Now they have your attention."

"Dude," Fleck snapped. "Why are you defending them?"

"I'm not," I replied. "I'm just trying to give my view of what is happening. They aren't hurting her. Not Katie."

"She's so young." Nila folded her arms tight to her body. "Can you imagine what she was feeling when that all happened. How scared she was. Bella..." Nila walked over to her. "Did she fight or scream, was she scared? Tell me."

"Nila," Bella spoke slightly frightened. "I kept trying to tell you..."

Fleck whistled short and sweet. He stood by the window. "We have company."

143

I hurried over and peeked out. A black SUV was parked by the gate. A man in a suit, looking like some sort of CIA agent, stepped from the driver's side.

Then I watched her get out of the car as well, dressed as if going to a business meeting.

"Who is that?" Nila asked. "She looks familiar."

"Almada Hillgrove," I answered. "She took over when Clare was killed."

Nila wasn't strong, I saw it and knew it, but it didn't stop her from grabbing the door, swinging it open, and pulling out her pistol as she raged to the front gate.

I handed June to Bella. "Can you watch her?" Without waiting for an answer from her, I hurried behind Nila, as did Fleck and Ben.

"Where is my daughter!" Nila blasted.

I could see the CIA looking guy had a shoulder harness, but he didn't pull it. Almada lifted her hands.

"Where?" Nila repeated.

"Mrs. Carter," Almada said softly. "We are not here to play wild west with you. I'm not armed and Jason doesn't even have his hand on his weapon."

"Again, I'll ask." Nila walked to the fence. "Where is my daughter?"

"I think we both know the answer to that," Almada replied. "She is with us. Safe and sound and in good hands."

"I want her back...now."

"We are on a cusp, a complete cusp of a breakthrough. Your daughter is right now one of a kind and I mean that. She is special and we need her. We waited until we absolutely needed her. We could have come sooner."

"You took her without permission."

"I know you feel that way…"

"What! How can you…"

"Can you please calm down?"

"Lady," Fleck said. "You blasted in here, knocked us all out, and kidnapped a kid."

"It's in national interest. It would be in global interest if we could reach beyond the continent. We can't," Almada replied. "Besides, would you have willingly handed her over? Would you have come to the Colony Alpha? Reached out to us. No, you have hidden for months. What goes on beyond these fences is none of your concern. You don't care."

Nila responded, "You got that right."

"Then I apologize for the means, but it will justify the end." She smiled. "She's your daughter, I understand that. You, Nila, are welcome to come and see her, stay with her." She lifted her hand once more and reached into her jacket. She pulled out an envelope, rolled it up, and pushed it into the link of the fence. "That is where you can find us. We're not hiding. And we have something for you, Ben." Almada nodded at Jason. He walked to the SUV and reached into the back, then returned with a small green cooler bag. He tossed it over the fence and it landed by Fleck.

Fleck leaned down and lifted it.

"That is for you, doctor," Almada said. "Ben, we used something milder on Nila, I'm certain it isn't harmful, but you will want to flush her system as soon as possible to be sure. All you need is in that bag."

There was a strange, stunned look on Ben's face. He looked at Almada as if she knew something she shouldn't.

Almada smiled and stepped back. "We'll leave you be. You know where we are. But Nila, when you come. You come alone or…" She smiled and looked at me. "Captain Marshall. I do have to say, Captain, I had a feeling you were lying about her voice on the radio. I wasn't sure you knew where she was. Good thing for us you stole that radio. The GPS tracking on it went out until several weeks ago when you went to East Brady. Then we lost you again. I'm not surprised at all you're here."

She waved and walked back to the SUV.

"I'm coming for my daughter." Nila charged the fence.

"I'm sure. Then you'll thank us." She paused. "Maybe not you, but the young woman standing on the porch will." Saying no more, Almada got into the SUV.

I heard them pull away, but I had turned to look at Bella. She stepped off the porch. June ran to me, while Bella carried Christian. I wondered what Almada meant, I suppose we all did.

Nila walked to the fence, pulling the envelope and she paused.

"Give me that." Ben reached for the bag,

That was when I noticed Fleck staring me down.

"What?" I asked.

"You led them here," Fleck said.

"I did no such thing. Not on purpose."

"You knew they had heard Nila on the radio. Isn't that what she implied?"

"Why do I get this feeling you're getting really shitty with me?" I asked.

"Because I am."

"Enough," Ben said. "We need to get into the house. Nila? Nila?" He snapped his finger.

Nila turned slowly holding the envelope.

Fleck grew heated and moved toward me. "Wanna know what I think?"

"I'm pretty sure you'll tell me."

"Fleck!" Ben shouted.

"What?" Fleck snapped.

"Grab her."

A part of me believed Fleck was pretty close to decking me for some reason, had it not been for Ben. It was one of those crazy moments when I realized how well Ben knew Nila. Knew her so well that as a friend and a doctor he saw she was going down.

When he ordered Fleck to grab her it was just in the nick of time. Fleck turned and caught her before she hit the ground.

"Is she okay?" Bella asked, opening the door as Fleck carried Nila inside.

"Yes," Ben answered. "Fleck, put her in the bed."

"What's in the bag?" I asked.

Ben undid the zipper. "Just as I suspected, an IV."

"What the hell?" Fleck placed Nila on the bed. "Why would they bring one for her and not us?"

"Is it because she's a woman?" Bella asked. "Did they give her a man strength dart?"

"Something like that." Ben sat on the bed, feeling Nila's hand for a vein. "I'm going to need something to hang this IV bag with once I get the line started."

"You and I"— Fleck pointed at me—"are not done."

"I did not bring them here. I did not lead them," I defended.

"You expect us to believe that?" Fleck asked. "You show up, so do helicopters. She said you heard her on the radio."

"Yes, yes, I did." I noticed when I said that Ben glanced up at me. "But they asked me if it was her and I said it wasn't. I didn't want them to find her if she didn't want found."

"But you did," Fleck stated. "You wanted to find her."

"I wanted to find a place. I have not lied to any of you."

"Where's your radio?" Fleck asked me.

"What?"

"Fleck," Bella tried to interject.

"Where is your radio?"

"It's in my things. I haven't touched it since East Brady," I said. "And you're accusing me for no reason."

"I have plenty of reason," Fleck argued.

"Will you two…" Ben stood up and handed the IV bag to Fleck. "Hold this while I find something to secure it."

Fleck took the bag as Ben walked out. "Get the radio, Sean. If you want us to trust you, hand it over."

"Fleck," Bella said. "Listen—"

"You know what?" I said. "If it makes you feel better, I will. Okay. You can have it." I walked out of Nila's bedroom and went to the back room where June and I slept. Immediately I reached for the top of my dresser. It wasn't there. I swore I put it there. I checked my drawers, the nightstand. Maybe it was in the car. I hated going back to tell Fleck that. I was certain he was going to come up with a reason why I was some sort of traitor.

I headed back to Nila's bedroom. Ben had returned and was duct taping the IV bag to a broom handle.

Fleck held out his hand. "Where is it?"

"It's not in my room, I must have put it somewhere else," I replied. "I'll find it."

Fleck tossed up his hands. "Am I the only one here who thinks this is all on him?"

"Guys," Bella spoke up. "I have to—"

"Hold on, Bella," Ben said and looked at Fleck. "I understand why you think that way, but I don't think so."

Fleck laughed in ridicule. "How can you say that? They tracked him. And I think he communicated with them. How else do you explain why they easily found that hatch? They wouldn't know it was there if someone didn't tell them. Imagine Katie, as tough as she is, she's a kid. Probably crying and screaming, not knowing..."

"She wasn't crying," Bella said. "They opened the hatch and she went without a fight."

"Wh...what?" Fleck asked. "Okay, maybe she wasn't scared. Someone told them about the hatch."

"I agree," Ben said.

"Ben," I spoke up. "I swear..."

Ben stopped me by holding up his hand. "Someone did communicate with them. I don't think it was you, Sean. Not only did they know about the hatch...this"—he pointed to the IV—"they said the tranquilizer was safe but to flush it out of her...they knew she was pregnant. None of you did. Did you?"

"She's pregnant?" Fleck asked.

I shook my head. "I had no idea."

"She didn't want anyone to know. But someone did," Ben said. "The Colony isn't psychic."

"Guys!" Bella spoke loudly. "I have been trying to tell you and no one will let me speak. I think I know who was

149

radioing them." She reached for her back pocket and handed Ben my radio.

"What the hell?" Fleck snapped.

Almost bashful, Bella brought her shoulders up. "I tried to tell Nila, all of you. It wasn't me. But that was in the hatch."

"That's what I thought." Ben sighed, tapping the radio on his hand. "Katie."

SEVENTEEN

COMING TO GRIPS

Nila

The colors were muted, more like sepia. The same look seen in an old photograph that had faded and lost its luster. I knew with every ounce of my being it was a dream. I felt it, I sensed it. I was knowledgeable, lucid in that dream, and at any point it could tip and I would wake up.

Many times I had fallen asleep with the television on, and whatever show was playing made its way somehow into my dreams. This was the same thing.

In the distance muffled, I could hear Ben and Fleck. Though I couldn't understand what they were saying.

I was somewhere else, in a dream. While it looked dark, it was a place I longed to go.

In my father's kitchen, the home where I grew up. Katie was giggling. But she was younger, maybe three.

"Come on, Mummy." She giggled and ran, her voice echoed.

I followed, holding out my hand, wanting her to take it. She raced through the living room and I froze. My father sat in his recliner, legs extended.

"Move will ya, Nillie, The Steelers are about to kick a field goal."

There was more of a reverb to his voice, a memory playing back, grabbed from the banks of my mind.

"Yes, Dad," I replied, stepping aside and staring at him.

"Mummy! Come on." Katie raced out the front door. I wanted to just stay and look at my father. He looked perfect and healthy, but the dream portion of my mind reasoned Katie shouldn't be outside alone.

I floated in my steps, pressing on air as I walked outside.

Everything was overexposed and lacked even more color. Katie ran across the yard to the house next door.

Lev's father's house.

I felt it in my chest as I walked in. It was dark in there, dismal almost. She held out her little hand and smiled. She had bangs, I remembered when I cut them like that.

Another childish giggle and her fingers gripped mine.

A song began to play, some country tune I wasn't familiar with. It was loud and Katie gripped my other hand.

"Let's do Ring Around the Rosie," she said, her voice bouncing in some sort of echo chamber.

Katie pulled on my arms and moved in a circle.

One circle, two…I felt dizzy…three.

On the third spin she released my hands. I finished the turn not only facing a bright and vivid living room, but I saw him standing at the door.

Lev.

His giant frame taking up most of the door.

I physically felt my heart pound in that dream when he looked over his shoulder at me.

"Lev." I rushed to him.

"Nila."

I reached for him. His voice wasn't like Katie's or my dad's, it was normal.

"Nila." He grabbed my hand. "What are you doing here?"

I looked down to his fingers. I could feel them, so real.

"Oh, God, Lev. I miss you so much."

"I know. But you cannot be here. It is not the place or time."

"I can't leave," I said. "I can't walk away."

"Sometimes you must. You need to step away for the better, for the good."

"What does that mean?"

"You'll know. Right now...you need to go."

"One more minute. I just..." I brushed my thumb against his hands. "One more minute."

"No." He shook his head, then looked directly at me. It was his eyes, I felt his soul at that second. He leaned down close, and I even swore I could smell him, feel his breath as he brought his lips near my ear. "It's not time yet. Let me go, Nila." He tried to pull his hand away. "Let me go."

"No, Lev."

"Nila." Again, he pulled back and locked into a stare. "You need to go."

I hated the feeling when he removed his hand from mine. The coarseness of his skin, brushing against my fingers, and when he released, I fell back.

An enormous pressure filled my chest, all air escaped my body and I sat straight up, wheezing in as if I had to refill my lungs.

My entire body trembled and shook. Heart racing, I swing my legs over the bed.

153

Was it a dream? Was it some sort of out of body experience? Whatever it was felt so real, I still felt as if I were there.

There was a light on in my bedroom and a glass of water on my nightstand. I downed it and felt it hit my stomach with a knot.

I wondered if I had been sleeping very long; it seemed darker out. But then I heard the sound of thunder.

A storm had rolled in. The thought of that sickened me, because I knew it would make getting to Katie harder.

Voices of everyone carried to me and I stood from the bed. I felt better, less out of it than I felt after I was hit with that dart.

An empty IV bag hung on a broom by my bed. The line no longer running to me, it just dangled there, but the little needle thing was still taped to my arm.

I felt useless and like a horrible mother. How could I sleep so long when my child was helpless, out there and alone?

I followed the voices to the kitchen. Maybe one of them would help me figure out how to get Katie.

They were sat at the table with what looked like a pot of soup in the middle, and they all looked up when I walked in.

"Nila," Ben said. "How are you feeling?"

"Good. I died."

Everyone responded with a shocked, "What!"

"I mean, I think I did. For a minute." I pulled out a chair and sat down. "I'm almost positive. Because I saw Lev."

"Oh, whew," Fleck said with some relief. "You had me scared until you said you saw Lev. You always see Lev."

"Not like this. What happened to me?" I asked Ben.

"The tranquilizer was too much for you," Ben answered. "Do you remember them giving me a little cooler sack?"

I nodded.

"It had an IV. To push that through your system," Ben replied.

"That's odd. Why would they do that?"

"You're pregnant," Fleck said. "Which you never told us. Here I just thought you were putting on weight."

"How far along are you?" Sean asked. "If you don't mind me asking."

"Not far," I replied.

Ben added, "I calculated fifteen weeks. A little over three months."

"You're in your second trimester already?" Sean asked.

Fleck scoffed a little laugh. "Look at you throwing out big words like you're an expert."

"Trimester is not a big word," Sean said. "And I am kind of. I have two kids. Well, they passed, but I have them always."

"Sorry, man," Fleck said. "You never said anything. I didn't know."

"It's painful," Sean replied.

"Wait a second." I glanced over at Ben. "They gave an IV for me specifically?"

Ben nodded.

"Like they knew I was pregnant?" I shook my head in disbelief. "How in the world would they know I was pregnant? That had to be by chance."

"We don't think so." Ben stood up and walked to the counter by the sink. He returned and placed Sean's radio on the table. "I think there's something you need to know."

It was almost emotionally devastating to hear that my five-year-old child could have been responsible for bringing the raid on the camp.

Actually, it was inconceivable to me. How would she even know to do that? I knew she was bright and spending all that time with adults thrust her into another level, but to do so intentionally was a lot to deal with.

It was hard to believe.

But then again, knowing the radio had GPS, all she had to do was turn it on. All anyone had to do was turn it on.

It could have been anyone at the cabin, but the fact The Colony knew I was pregnant left me, Ben, and Katie. Although never confirmed to my daughter, I knew she knew. Just by the crackers left at my bedside in the morning.

The storm made getting a radio call out nearly impossible. I wanted to reach out to The Colony to see if talking to them was possible. Plus, I needed to check on my daughter.

Finally around nine p.m., we got through on the big radio.

They put me through to Dr. Hillgrove who told me that Katie was absolutely fine and they would get her to talk to me.

Before that though, I had to ask, "Was my daughter the one that led you to us?"

When she confirmed she was, I went into denial. Arguing it was impossible, but within a few minutes, she played me a confirmation recording.

Because, as Dr. Hillgrove said, they knew I would never believe it unless I heard with my own ears.

Sean confirmed they recorded radio messages.

I got more of a confirmation than I was ready for.

156

"Katie," my daughter said. "Who is…"

"Katie," Dr. Hillgrove said. "Katie, you need to press the button when you talk. Hold it."

"Okay. That man is nice. He said you wanted to talk to me."

"Yes, he is, and I did. Katie, you know how special you are."

"Mommy tells me that all the time."

"Katie, do you want the monsters to go away?"

"You mean the dead people?" asked Katie. "Yes."

"Katie, you can make it stop. We need your help, Katie. When we're ready will you help us?"

"Will my mommy be mad?"

"How can she get mad at you for being a hero?"

At first I thought it was total manipulation of a child. I was angry, then they told me Katie had been radioing for weeks. Sean didn't use the radio, he never bothered with it, and never knew it was gone.

"I'm sorry, everyone, I am really sorry," I told them as they gathered around the back room. "I don't understand her."

"Join the club," Fleck commented. "That kid never had a filter. I don't think she ever will."

"Mommy," Katie's voice came over the radio.

I spun and picked up the microphone. "Baby, hey, baby are you okay?"

"I'm fine, Mommy. I had spaghetti tonight. Almie made it."

"Who is Almie?"

Katie giggled. "The pretty doctor lady. I'm staying with her, Mommy. My room is so pretty."

"That's good. Are you scared?" I asked.

"No. I didn't like when they took my blood. But I know it's to help people. I'm sorry, Mommy, they shot you guys. I didn't want them to shoot you. They said they were just giving me a ride."

"I know, Katie. They probably told you lots of things."

"Are you mad at me?"

"Katie…Katie, why did you call them on the radio? Why did you take the radio?"

"I was playing with it," replied Katie. "Hitting the button and singing and some man came on. He was nice. Then Almie talked to me. She was nice."

"But you didn't put the radio back."

"They said not to because Sean was a bad man," Katie replied.

"Fucking knew it," Fleck barked. "Even The Colony doesn't trust him."

"Give it a break," Sean retorted.

"Mommy, I have to go now. I want to watch a movie. They have movies here. Are you coming here? They said you will come."

"Yes, baby, I'll be there tomorrow."

It took a lot for me to end that radio call. Even though my daughter sounded fine and content, not frightened at all, I was a wreck.

She was out of my care, away from me and I hadn't been apart from my daughter for longer than eight hours in years. I wanted nothing more than to get in the car and go north the twenty-five miles. But I knew the dark, rainy weather, along with wet leaves and the dead would make that short journey treacherous.

First thing in the morning, I would be on my way. They had my child against my wishes, and cure to humanity, selfish or not, I wanted her back.

EIGHTEEN

HOME BODY

Sean
September 21

The first day of fall made its presence known. The wind was strong and chilled, a mist of rain just made everything cold and damp. And the gray skies didn't help the prospect of the trip to Colony Alpha seem any better.

It felt like we were going to a funeral instead of finding and getting Katie.

Almada informed us that the roadways were clear and the dead would be minimal. Then again, it was only twenty-five miles. Once off the mountain, it was a trip that would take a short time.

We were never really close to finding it at any point, either, while searching for Meg or just supplies. We never went outside the twenty-mile radius.

The cleared pathway wasn't an indication they were close because Fleck and Nila had seen them headed north, plowing the highway as they went.

If we had only gone a bit further we would have known for sure.

Nila was up at the crack of dawn waiting and willing to go. Almada asked if she wouldn't come until after nine because they wanted to run some tests and feed Katie.

Nila agreed to not arrive at the gates until then, but that wasn't stopping her from leaving early.

She would just wait outside.

I thought a lot about the fact that she recruited just me to go. Not that I wouldn't under other circumstance, but I was fearful of going because of June. I wasn't worried about getting hurt or killed on the way there, I was worried what would happen to me once I arrived.

I wasn't sure what the laws were with The Colony on defectors, but I didn't want to find out.

Plus…June.

Had I not had her, then I wouldn't hesitate, but that little girl had become my buddy and my second lease on life. She was happy, she smiled, and while she didn't replace my own daughter, she was helping me heal.

There were pictures of her family in the bag I grabbed near her father's body. Other than her father, I didn't know who they were, but that didn't stop me from making those photos our nightly routine.

Showing them to her, guessing who the people were. Just keeping her familiar with those she loved and lost and those who loved her so very much.

If something were to happen to me, who would do that with her?

And there was also the fact that I trusted no one with her safety. If I knew we were going to be gone just a couple of hours, that would be one thing, but there was no guarantee when we arrived that we weren't walking into some sort of trap and suddenly we were prisoners.

It was on my mind heavily and I felt like a coward, but I couldn't go and I had to tell her.

I just couldn't leave June.

When I returned to the cabin, she was in the kitchen with Ben and Fleck.

"Look Sean." Nila held up a bag. "Peanut butter sandwiches. In case we're stuck there and they don't feed us."

"Always good to be prepared," Ben said.

"Plus, she does eat a lot," Fleck added. "So keep her fed so she doesn't get miserable."

"My wife used to get so mad," I said. "She'd want something, swear she was starving for it, and when I'd get it, she'd take two bites and that was it."

"I was like that with Addy," Nila told me. "Now, you know, I think Lev's baby is gonna be like Lev, consume a lot of food and a lot of space. At least…" She exhaled. "I'm not hiding it anymore. You okay?"

"Look, don't hate me," I said.

"Too late," Fleck retorted.

"Nila, I want to help, but I don't want to leave June. I know the chances are we'll be right back, but we don't know for certain. I defected, I took things. I finally have a purpose again in June and…"

"Say no more." Nila held up her hand. "I completely understand and get it."

"Someone has to go with her," Fleck said.

"What does someone have to go with me?" Nila asked.

"To protect you."

162

Nila laughed. "Oh my God, you're funny. I can protect myself."

"Not when you're pregnant."

"I can still protect myself."

"Not that you can't," said Ben, "but you shouldn't go alone."

"I know Almada said you alone or you go with me," I said. "You radioed this morning, is there anyone else they'd let go?"

"Yeah," Nila answered. "Actually, they did."

"I'll go," Fleck said.

"No." Nila shook her head. "They specifically said not you."

"What? What did I do?" Fleck asked shocked.

"They said Ben would do." Nila glanced at Ben. "Will you?"

"Sure, I'll go. If…if Sean and Fleck promise to watch Sawyer. Bella has her handful with Christian."

"Man," Fleck said. "It's kid mountain. So I'm a babysitter."

"No," Nila replied. "You're going to make sure everything stays safe. Sean can be the kid wrangler."

"I have no problem with that."

"But all this Plan B stuff," Nila said. "We'll be back by lunch, and I'll be back with my daughter."

I gave a grateful smile for her being completely understanding and not treating me as if I were shucking some manly responsibility. I had no doubt there would be no problems if she went without me. I did, however, doubt the ease of how things would go.

Nila was confident.

I kept my mouth shut because I wasn't. The Colony wanted Katie…nothing was going to go smoothly.

NINETEEN

GO AND CHOOSE

Nila

It was evident no one from The Colony was from the local area or remotely from Eastern Pennsylvania. Their choice to clear the main highway, at least for us, took us out of our way.

We took Route Eight north as far as we could, but a massive pileup near Interstate Eighty had us backtracking and taking back roads.

There were a lot of dead wandering the wreckage. I couldn't figure out what they were looking for. Ben suggested maybe someone was hiding out there.

Sticking around was not an option.

The dead weren't gone, they were still gathering in numbers and that made me nervous.

When would they ever go away?

They went in cycles. Sick then infected and raging, to deaders who slowly decomposed until they were nothing to fear but crawling bodies of deteriorating flesh and tendons.

Pathetic and sad.

Crawling, falling apart until they just stopped and the brain finally rotted to the point they were finally done.

Then it started again.

Like the seasons.

It cycled through. Was it the way life would be from here on in? Chipping away at humanity until we were all gone.

That was the only positive thing I could think of that The Colony was doing. I truly believed they were trying to solve it. Until they did, we faced another winter.

The first winter had been interesting at the cabin. We had stocked up on food, wood and were ready for it.

Then the first winter never came.

Some cold blew in, a bit of ice here and there, but no big snowfall. Nothing like we used to get and nothing that lasted. Hunting wasn't as good as we'd hoped only when the short bursts of snow came, otherwise the animals were snatched by the dead. Then the deer, like the human population, were safe. Well, the deer were at least safe from the dead. They were as much dinner as we were.

We all had bets on what would happen to the deaders once winter blew in full force.

Fleck and I believed they would freeze and pause, Lev thought it wouldn't make a difference because it wouldn't get that cold, and Ben as a doctor totally believed they would just slow down.

Of course we had to see. So, we kept two deaders, one female and petite, and a larger man. It took a while for us to find recently transition deaders. Ones that had just turned from being infected.

It was something to do and it was fun, as twisted as it seemed.

Sure enough, once the snow finally came, they were like monuments. Barely moving, barely moaning, frozen. They didn't generate any heat to melt the snow, so they were like patio furniture, collecting the mounds of white and even when the sun came out it didn't melt.

But once it truly stopped snowing and the temperatures of February crept up into the upper thirties, they revived.

If that was the case again, winter would be safe. Ben was right on one point: when the temperature dropped, even without snow, the decomposition slowed down. While it made it safer for us, it prolonged their existence.

All that would be moot if The Colony cured the virus or found some sort of scientific defensive against it.

A cure would cause it to stop. To fade out. No longer would people get sick or infected if bitten. Eventually, the dead would rot where they dropped like roadkill.

Ben and I didn't speak too much on the car ride there.

Maybe a comment here and there about the weather or a deader we saw.

However, as we neared where they set up the new colony, Ben and I did start talking again. Mainly about the choices they made in location.

Being that we were both from the state, we were familiar with the place.

They chose a location in a town we knew as Oil City. I didn't get it. Yeah, Oil City was a nice small town and like East Brady had a natural defense with the river, but Franklin was right down the road. And coming from the highway you had to drive through Franklin anyhow.

The nearest medical facility was in Seneca, so it made very little sense to me.

Then I knew when we pulled into Franklin why it was off the chart to be a Colony.

The world and its demise into the walking dead had not been kind to the charming town of Franklin. It was hard to discern what exactly was the cause, the dead or perhaps the living fighting back.

Not a single window on the picturesque business district was intact. Some of the buildings had been burned. On the sidewalk were mountains of trash bags and furniture and as we drove farther through town, we saw cleanup crews.

"Maybe this will also be part of The Colony," Ben said. "There's a reason they're cleaning it up."

"A lot of people would come through here. They wouldn't want those traveling to find The Colony to go through here like it is. Like going to Atlantic City. Ever drive there? It's bad on the way to the casinos."

"Can't say that I have. That's assuming they are recruiting residents."

"They are, they asked Huck."

"How many though? You have to assume a lot of Colony One residents may be waiting to move in here as well."

"Poor Meg, this is all she wanted. To be back in a community, to pretend that life was normal."

"It's not pretending, Nila." Ben glanced at me. "This is normal. Whether you barricade a town, live in a Colony or on a mountain, this is life now. No going back to normal because that's what normal is now."

The thought of, *Here we go again* went through my mind as soon as we reached the end point, a Holiday Inn in a town called Reno. It was tiny and sat on the river that wound through Oil City.

Like we had experienced months ago at Colony One, there we were made to abandon the car and check in our weapons. I was under the impression things weren't fully functioning. But they had their rules and I had mine.

"We're not staying," I told the man at check out. "Not for long. I'm here for my daughter and then we're leaving."

Ben whispered to me, "Was that the plan?"

"It is now," I replied.

The man at the front desk looked at me, then lifted a bin. "Check your weapons."

This time there was no blood test, no bands given to us or an examination. We passed through the Processing Center and were permitted through the fence into the area marked Colony Alpha.

Like the previous Colony, any and everything on the sides of the road between Reno and Oil City had been cleared and flattened. It was a three-mile stretch, a walk that took close to an hour for us.

I felt vulnerable, no weapon, no way to protect ourselves. Every quarter mile there was a Colony guard twiddling his thumbs or something like that. He'd acknowledge us as we passed. A lot of good they would do if there was a hoard of deaders.

But we didn't see any.

Finally we reached the limits of Colony Alpha, and along with a huge barricade and soldier present was that black SUV.

Standing by it was Almada.

She looked pleasant, dressed more casual, and she smiled at us like we were long lost pals.

"I'm glad you're here," she said. "We would have had a car waiting for you, but we didn't know when you'd arrive."

Ben held up the radio. "Really, because I thought this had GPS."

"No need to track it once we located it." She forced a smile. "Besides, healthy exercise is good for you, Nila."

"I don't mind. I do want my daughter."

"Yes, and you will see her..."

"Want her. I'm taking her."

"I know you feel strongly—"

I waved my hand to silence her. "That's an understatement. I want my daughter and I have every intention of taking her back with me."

"Of course, but I need you to know," Almada said, "we are not the bad guys here. I know it seems like it, but we're not. Before you take her, you're going to go on a little tour."

"Oh, I've been to Oil City lots of times," I said. "No need."

"But you've not been to Colony Alpha."

Ben asked, "Is this a trick?"

"Not at all." Almada shook her head. "I just want you to see the whole thing, hear me out before you leave. I give you my word if you let me take you around and explain things, you can walk out with Katie when we're done."

"My daughter is not a bartering tool."

"We're not bartering, I am asking."

"For what purpose?" I asked.

"In hopes you'll change your mind."

"About what? Taking my daughter?"

"No, about staying on. This way." Almada walked to the SUV and opened the back door.

Ben gently grabbed my arm stopping me. "So one time the wife and I went to Vegas and got roped into listening to a time share thing in order to get a free buffet and grand canyon tour."

"What does that have to do with anything?" I asked in a whisper.

"This feels like the same thing. Only the reward is your daughter. They'll give her up, but be prepared for high pressure."

"There's nothing, Ben, she can say or do to change my mind."

"I didn't say she would. Just…be prepared."

I understood what he meant. I got his analogy about the time share demonstration. I was certain Almada was going to tell me all the wonderful things, but I wondered why she'd even bother. I was positive I would leave the budding Colony Alpha with my daughter and nothing she said inside the walls would make a bit of difference to me.

Almada was without a doubt a post-apocalypse salesperson trying to sell us a spot in utopia.

Giving credit where credit was due, Oil City looked unscathed. The windows in the shops weren't broken, everything was clean and bright when we pulled into the business district and stepped out of the car.

"Not sure if you were aware, being so close, but Oil City was a stronghold. When we arrived there were about thirty residents who were alive and well," Almada explained. "They'd kept it up so our job was easier. We wanted a place called Evans City, but there was far too much to clean up in a time frame we'd given ourselves."

"Why are you the one running things?" I asked. "Aren't you a doctor or scientist?"

"Yes to both," she said. "And I am not the one running things. Not even close. I run the science division and health, but not all this. I'm with you because we know each other."

"You took my child."

"She wanted to come."

"She's five," I said. "If SpongeBob invited her to the ocean she'd jump right in."

"I think she's smarter than that. But she's your child, you know her best."

Ben asked, "How many people live here?"

"Right now? About four hundred. That's because we're in the building phase still. Trying to get power and resources ready for the winter. We hope to move a lot of Colony One people here. As of this moment they are spread out. They want to be reunited with their neighbors."

"Why are you doing this?" I asked. "I mean, you lost two Colonies. Both fell to the dead."

"And we'll keep building," she replied. "Not everyone wants to live off the land in a cabin in the woods. Not everyone wants to go back to the days of the settlers. You do. Many don't. They want comforts and security."

"It's a world of dead."

"Which we hope to change," she said. "We will change. Not hope. We will. Just because we lost our way of life doesn't mean we say screw it and just start from scratch or go back to basics. We can rebuild. We are already. Why do you think we have so many helping? It's not only something to do, but something to strive for." She looked at Ben. "Are you happy living in a cabin in the woods?"

"Yeah. I am. We're family there. It's good," Ben replied.

"Can you handle everything?" she asked.

"We try."

"You can't," I said. "The more people you have here, the more potential for problems, for a repeat of chaos and death. For the dead to make their way in. You had the dead in Colony One."

"A mistake we won't make again. We think we have learned this virus. Is there a chance? Yes. We could have an outbreak like in a local town here. But we know what to look for and hopefully isolate the sick before it spreads too far and fast. Before long, that won't even be a threat."

"So you have the cure?" Ben asked.

"Yes. We know how to beat it. Prevent it…well, not yet. We felt our priority had to be with curing it."

Admittedly, I didn't want to smile when I heard that, but I did. If they did beat it, if they did have the cure, another mother wouldn't have to lose a child. Someone wouldn't have to lose a person they loved.

Almada held out her hand. "All this is growing and we have a lot to do. I am optimistic about having it ready by December, but more than likely it won't be until spring."

"This is great, all that you're doing," I told her. "To each his own, but why are you wasting time trying to sell it to me?"

"We're not done. Not by a long shot, and we need your daughter," she replied.

"But we're twenty-five miles away. You have choppers. It's not like we will be thousands of miles from you."

"Nila," Almada said. "I want you to want to be here. To be part of this. Be a leader here like you are with your group. We need strong people, good shooters, and doctors." She looked at Ben. "We want Katie here. Twenty-four hours a day, seven days a week. Not to hook up to machines to be a lab experiment. But to be protected. She is one of a kind, the only person we have found. We need to keep her protected."

"I can protect her."

"Yes, you can. But we want you to protect her here, where you have back up, where she can be flown to safety on a moment's notice. And you're expecting, don't you want the best medical care? Ultrasound and a hospital to deliver."

"I have the best medical care." I glanced to Ben with a smile. "Now, Almada, this is nice and you guys are doing a great job. But it isn't for me or my daughter. Take me to her, so I can take her home."

The tour moved from the center of town, and we didn't make any more stops. Almada merely pointed out the window to show me things. We drove to the high school. It was also surrounded by a fence, and trailers were on the grounds. They looked like FEMA trailers, but I didn't see many people.

Almada explained the school was their research and medical center.

"We're still remodeling," she said as she led us down a hall. "We're getting there."

I grew impatient. "Where is Katie?"

"She's here. Once we get into my lab, I'll radio for her. She's with Samson, one of the lab techs. They're doing puzzles. She said she finds him fun. She can be a bit peculiar," Almada said. "We have the means for her to watch movies, play games, but she likes to draw. Strange drawings."

"She's gifted," I said.

"I know." Almada looked at me with a serious expression. Another turn down a hallway and she opened a door. "In here."

As soon as I stepped in, I could see that the classroom had been divided. A glass wall separated the room and computer monitors hung on the wall. As she said, she radioed for them to bring Katie.

"How often do you venture from your cabin?" Almada asked.

"A couple times a week," I replied. "But winter is coming so it will be less."

"Good, because the virus can live on a surface for up to ten days. Ten days, that is insane," she said. "Which means, you can pick it up anywhere. Animals carry it, dogs, birds, deer…you name it. The incubation period can be as long as another ten days before it's even detectable."

I tried not to let her see my face, but I immediately looked to Ben on that one.

"Our scans," she said, "detect it before any physical symptoms show, like the veins, which is the first telltale sign. I hate this virus, Nila. I want it defeated."

"And you think you can?" I asked.

"Yes. Yes." She nodded. "Again, we are not the bad guys here, this virus is. Katie is the key. Now realistically, we can't get enough antibodies from her to save the world. We're in the phase where we are trying to replicate what she naturally makes. I don't want to take any blood or plasma from her less than a week apart."

"Can I bring her here once a week?" I asked. "I want this beat as well, I'm just not willing to give up my daughter."

"You don't have to give up your daughter. Move here with her, work with us," Almada said.

"And give up my cabin, which is my father's and has been our saving grace."

"Nila, that cabin may have been your saving grace, but it can be your death sentence. Bring your people here. If they get ill, they have first priority to the cure. I can and will promise you that. If one person in your camp gets it, without the cure, they all will die."

Ben spoke up. "If those who are susceptible don't leave the cabin, then they aren't at risk."

"You don't think?" Almada retorted. "Ask East Brady. They don't know how they got it. Ask me." She cocked back with arrogance. "I don't know how I caught it either."

"You caught the virus?" I asked.

"Yes," she replied. "I was the first human subject. What did I have to lose? It was a month ago."

Almada leaned over and clicked on the keyboard of the computer. The first image that popped up was of an ankle, the smallest bit of black capillaries could be seen. "That's my foot. The day I saw. Now day two…" She changed the picture. The veins had moved up her leg and another picture showed them under the arm. "Day three." She changed it again. The veins from the arms had spread to the neck. "About that point I felt a little ill, not much. That is the day I had the injection. Day four." The picture looked as if it didn't change until she switched to the next one. They were predominantly lighter. "Day five." Again, she clicked until she went through a series of pictures where no veins were present. "It took until day eight for the veins to disappear. I felt better on day four; however, I was still contagious until day seven. And that is my concern. Different people have different reactions."

"How so?" Ben questioned.

"I was fortunate enough to have a slower moving virus. I have seen people go from having no symptoms to transitioning into the rage phase in three days. The average I've seen is five days pre-symptoms to the point of no return."

I could tell by the look on Ben's face he was thinking of Lev. Like I was. Lev went from zero to sixty at an exuberant pace.

Ben questioned further. "Is it like a shot of penicillin, it gets rid of it, but no immunities?

"No, at least at this time we don't think it's a one shot treatment," Almada answered. "I still have antibodies. I'm not sure if we can catch it twice. There are several of us that are willing to volunteer."

"That's insane," Ben said.

"That's science now. That is why Katie is so vital."

"I'm not holding her back from helping," I replied. "I'm really not. I was going to, but I see why you need her."

"And it isn't just drawing a tiny tube a week to make serum. I'd have her protected like Fort Knox."

"I understand that."

Almada nodded. "At least you'll bring her here. I would think, at least in your condition, you'd want to make sure you're safe. Katie told me Lev died of the virus. Is he the father?"

I wanted to snap and say that was personal, but I didn't. I answered honestly.

"The child may not be immune. Right now it is protected by your antibodies and…" She stopped talking and must have noticed the look on my face and my reaction.

I had exhaled a shivering breath.

"What is it?" she asked.

I didn't want to tell her, but for the baby, for me, I needed to know. "You said…you said someone can have the infection in them days before it is detected by your scan. Have you done any studies at all on conceiving to someone infected?"

"So you think Lev was infected."

"I don't know. It was like five days later that the scan showed he was infected. Before he even showed any symptoms. So I don't know. According to you, there's a chance he was."

"There's a chance, yes. There's no study and no precedence, unless…unless you want to be that study."

I chuckled in disbelief. "In exchange for my daughter."

"In exchange for science."

There was that word again, she tossed it out science left and right. "I don't think—"

"What…" Ben interrupted. "What would that entail?"

"Ben?" I asked.

"Amniocentesis. Obviously after fourteen weeks."

"Which she is."

"That would give us the best indication."

I asked, "What if the baby isn't immune?"

"Then that baby would get the serum when he or she is born. That would be about the best we can do, and it would help other women to know as well," Almada replied. "Your help would be of immense service."

"So you want me to help build this place, give up my daughter, my body—"

"Nila," Ben stopped me. "She's offering help."

"They took my daughter, Ben. Took her. Stormed in like Normandy beach, took us all out and snatched her up," I argued. "I can't trust them."

"I think," Ben replied, "you should consider that you may not have a choice."

"Why are you so for this?" I asked.

"Because I'm a doctor, Nila and I love you and Katie, and I loved Lev. I want the best for your baby. In this world, right now, we are able to know if the baby is immune or not. If this wasn't an option for us, we wouldn't know anything when that child is born." He faced Almada. "Do you have the equipment to do this? I have never done one. Have you?"

"No."

"See." I laughed.

"But we have several obstetricians that have. I can have one here from Colony Three in a couple days. Think about it. Let me know and when you bring Katie in next week, we can take care of things for you."

"I'll think about it." I shifted my eyes to Ben. "Only because my doctor thinks it's a good idea."

Ben reached over and laid his hand on my back. "Good. Thank you."

"Now where is Katie?"

"I'm sure she'll be here any minute," Almada replied. "Last night she wouldn't go to sleep until she finished her drawing. Nila…you said she was special."

"She is."

"Do you believe that she is gifted?"

"Like smart or artistic?" I asked.

"No, like knowing things."

"Boy, you know, you toss the word science out all the time, are you telling me you think she knows things?" I questioned.

"I do. There are some things that science can't explain. That is one of them. My question is do you think she knows things?"

"I…I guess I do. She says things that she can't know," I answered. "It might be luck. I don't know. Why?"

"Because she did something that sent a chill up my spine when I showed her the doses of serum that she helped make."

"What did she do?"

Before Almada could answer, I heard the running feet and my daughter's bright voice when she ran into the room. "Mommy! Ben!"

I spun around. "Honey," I gushed and grabbed on to her. "Oh my gosh. I missed you."

"I missed you, too."

"Are you okay?"

"Yes. I was doing puzzles. You want to see my room?"

"Not right now, sweetie, we're going back to the cabin."

"We'll be back though."

"We will," I told her. "I promised that we'd help them."

"But I won't have the same room," she said. "Almada said I'll have a different room, just as pretty, but in our own place."

"What do you mean?"

"When we live here for a while."

"Katie, sweetie, we aren't living here."

Ben added, "We're just gonna come back once a week for them to do their test."

"Okay. Can Almie make me spaghetti? It was very good."

Almada smiled. "I will have it for you when you come back next week."

"Thank you." She held her hand to me to take. "Oh, Mommy, did she show you the box of medicine that will fix the sick?"

"No, she didn't."

"It's our box, Mommy."

"What are you talking about? The medicine is for people who are sick or get sick, like Lev and Meg."

Almada cleared her throat to grab my attention. She walked to a small refrigerator and opened it. When she turned around she held a case. "This is what I was telling you." Opening the small case, she reached in and lifted a rack. In the rack were six vials and the moment I saw then, I knew what Almada meant. A chill raced up my spine and I felt instantly sick to my stomach.

It was Katie's handwriting that labeled each vial. Even though a couple of the names were misspelled, it was abundantly clear who they were labeled for.

Ben. Sawyer. Fleck. Bella, June, Christian.

I lifted my eyes to Almada.

"They're ours, Mommy." Katie grabbed my hand. "I told her we will move here if we have to use them."

"We won't, Katie."

"Let's go home. I want to tell Fleck."

Ben coughed to clear his throat. "Well, I'm sure Fleck is going to be excited to hear that."

Katie led the way, nearly pulling me. I glanced back at Almada.

She lifted her head. "Think about the testing. I'll talk to you soon. My car will take you back."

"Yeah," I muttered still in shock, my head spinning. "I'll talk to you soon."

Katie was bright and bubbly, swinging my arm as she walked down the hall. Happy and in her own world. While I was grateful to have my daughter in my clutches, my mind kept going back to those vials and something Almada said when she arrived at our gate.

I stopped walking. "Katie, stay with Ben."

"Where are you going?"

"I need to talk to Almada."

"She's nice."

"I'm sure."

"Nila?" Ben looked at me with question.

"I'll be right back." Leaving them in the hall I returned to Almada's office. The door was still open and she was returning the vials to the fridge. I knocked on the door frame. "Can I ask you something?"

She shut the fridge and turned around. "Sure."

I stepped in. "When you came to my cabin, when you showed up like the CIA right after you kidnapped Katie, you said something. You said I wouldn't thank you, but the young woman on the porch would. I thought it was weird, but now…"

"Bella? Is that her name?" Almada asked.

"Yes."

"When we talked to Katie on the radio and told her how special she was, that she could help save sick people, she said…she said good because Bella was going to get sick and die first."

Slowly, I nodded. "Thank you. That's what I thought."

"Do you believe her?" Almada asked. "Katie and her thoughts, predictions, whatever you want to call them?"

"I don't know. I don't."

"Maybe a better question should be…do you want to take a chance on not believing them?"

"My answer will be the same, I don't know," I replied. We looked at each other in silence. I felt confused, almost in a dreamlike state. I didn't trust her, no matter how sincere she sounded. A part of me thought it was all one big mind game to get me and Katie to stay there. I just didn't under-stand what they could do to keep my child safe that I couldn't. There was no convincing me of that.

"It's a hard call, she's young," Almada said. "So it makes sense that you don't know. I don't know."

"I do know this, I have faith that I am doing all I can to keep my people safe. No one got sick when Lev was infected, and no one got sick when Meg had it. God willing, no one will get it now." I projected that confidently, gave her a nod of farewell, then left the office to take my daughter home.

TWENTY

THREE THINGS

Sean

Staying behind at the cabin with Fleck was one of the most tense situations of my life. Not that an apocalypse with the risen dead wasn't stressful, but more on a small scale, an interpersonal level. It felt as if every word I said would be met with attack, and any move I made would cause suspicion. I hated second guessing myself. I was not the reason the Colony of Hillgrove blasted the cabin.

After I made radio contact with Huck to let him know we no longer had to play the game of 'bad dialect,' I made lunch for the kids and even included Fleck.

He wouldn't touch it, which bred a small conversation.

"You know, you need to grow up," I told him.

"Maturity has nothing to do with trust."

"You don't think?"

I went back to minding my own business, playing with the kids. At least Bella was happy about it. She enjoyed the break from Christian.

She was an impressive young woman. No older than fifteen or sixteen, yet by what I had seen, she completely took over the mother role of Christian. She was good. I guess I was used to seeing teenagers being teenagers ... or acting like Fleck.

It felt like it was taking forever for Nila and Ben to get back. I tried reaching them with my radio but there was no answer.

So I worried.

What if it was a ruse and they weren't returning Katie? What if they just kept Nila and Ben? My mind raced with ways to pull off a rescue mission. Then I went into a phase where I blamed myself for not going. How my concern about not coming back for June was possibly cowardly.

June didn't have me for two years of her life, she would do just fine without me.

It was more for me than her.

It was too cold to take the kids out to play. Not that the fall weather was bitter cold, it wasn't, but I didn't see a coat for any of them.

I made a mental note that was going to be what we searched for on the next supply run.

Since a decent conversation with Fleck was out of the question, to pass the time, I decided to clean up. The cabin wasn't bad, just cluttered. Sawyer was the tidiest kid I'd ever met in my life. He was very organized in everything he did, from Legos to action figures. He kept them neatly in a box in the corner of the living room. That wasn't all that caught his attention.

Nila's father had a closet full of board games and puzzles. It was very telling the type of world we lived in before the dead rose, because Sawyer and Katie were obsessed with those puzzles like it was something new, a video game or something.

One thing that hadn't changed in the world was a child's ability to leave crayons and markers everywhere when they drew. My kids used to do the same thing.

Katie was no exception.

On the far end of the kitchen, on the floor no less, was her own personal messy art studio. I gathered the crayons and markers, putting them in the case. I then decided to gather her art.

Artistically, the pictures were like that of any other five-year-old. Her talent for lines or people wasn't excelled. However, her subject matter seemed a little skewed.

"Hey, Fleck," I called him, holding a picture. "Do you own a black tee shirt with a weird skull on it?"

"Why?'

"Can you answer the question?"

"Yep, my Punisher shirt. No, you cannot have it."

"I think Katie drew a picture of you."

If I ever had a doubt that Fleck was egotistical, that flew out the window as soon as he excitedly came to the kitchen.

"Let me see. I knew she liked me," he said.

"Um…that's still debatable." I handed him the drawing.

"What the fuck?" Fleck asked. "What's wrong with my eyes, and what is that on my face and hands? It looks like blood."

"I think it's supposed to be blood. See…" I pointed. "It's all over the floor. I think she drew you as a deader. If I'm not mistaken that is Ben you are eating."

"What the hell is the matter with her?"

Both of us looked at that picture together and turned in surprise when the door opened.

"I'm back!" Katie called out cheerfully.

"Everything okay?" Ben asked as he walked in.

Fleck held up the picture. "Katie, did you draw me as a deader?"

"I did. But don't worry, Fleck." She hugged his legs. "It won't happen now."

"That's good to know."

"Do you like it?" Katie asked.

"Actually, no, but that doesn't mean it isn't good."

I walked away from them to the living room. "Ben, everything go alright?"

"Yep." He glanced at Nila. "Pretty simple. We're going to take Katie back once a week so they can keep working. It's pretty much a cure."

A smile crept across my face. "They cured it? That's great news."

"It is but," Ben said, "they can't mass produce until they can replicate what they make from Katie's antibodies. Just a matter of time though."

I noticed Nila hadn't said anything. She slowly hung up her jacket. "Nila, are you okay?"

She nodded a 'hmm-hmm' and I walked toward her, too. "Just tired. I'm gonna lay down." She walked in and closed the door to her bedroom.

"She's fine." Ben tapped me on the shoulder as he moved by me. "Don't worry about it."

What choice did I have but to take his word for it? And really, worried or not, was it my business anyhow? For the time being I would let it go, and I went back to doing what I did before they came home.

The same as always.

Life in the cabin.

We did pretty much nothing.

Information overload.

As the day progressed, I learned a lot from Ben as to what happened at The Colony. More than just nothing.

Nila had a lot on her mind, but in my opinion not enough to warrant her staying in her room all day.

Then it was a medical lesson for all when she emerged from the bedroom.

Like the Ghostbusters using a PKE meter looking for spirits, Nila whipped out a scanner. The ones used on the highway and on people entering a Colony.

Apparently, Dr. Hillgrove gave her one before she left. Not even Ben knew. He said Nila went back to talk to Almada, she came out but Almada called her back again.

Fleck made a comment that it was a typical female thing, never able to just leave a place without a long, drawn-out goodbye.

Not wanting to be labeled misogynistic like Fleck, I kept my mouth shut, but I kind of agreed.

She announced, "Okay, here's the deal," as she held up the scanner. "This will be a daily occurrence. Every day. Just to be on the safe side."

"So you're gonna scan our necks and face?" asked Fleck.

"And arm pits. Dr. Hillgrove said ninety-nine percent of the virus starts as a viral infection in the"—she glanced down to her notes—"posterior auricular, posterior cervical or sub-capsular lymph nodes."

Everyone looked at her.

Ben clarified, "Behind the ear, side of neck, and armpit."

Fleck gave a thumbs-up. "Gotcha, that's why they scan the face. Why the hands?"

Nila furrowed her brow. "She didn't explain that."

I knew the answer. "In case it entered the hands through a small cut or hangnail. Like hand, foot and mouth. I scanned a lot of people and I don't think I ever saw it start on the hands."

"Yeah, so, everyone line up," Nila told us and then one by one, she did the same routine I had done many times. "Will I see?" she asked me.

"Yeah, you'll see," I told her. "No mistake."

She was thorough and then just to be safe, because there was a small chance, she made Ben, Fleck and Bella, check their groin area.

"What am I looking for?" Fleck asked, holding out the waist to his pants while shinning the scanner down.

Nila stifled a laugh. "If you don't know, I can't tell you."

He didn't get her attempt at humor, not one little bit.

After supper, Nila's mood was better. It was evident something was said at The Colony that made her worry about the ones that weren't immune.

I wanted to talk to her, to find out if there was more said than Ben had told us.

June was restless and it took forever to put her down. Even reading to her didn't help, which I didn't get. My kids used to be out like a light when I read.

Maybe my voice worked on everyone else, because when I emerged from the back bedroom, it was quiet and I had a feeling that everyone was sleeping. But the smell of fresh coffee told me someone was awake. Noticing the powdered creamer was out, it could be only one person...Nila.

I poured a cup for myself and headed to see if she was up in her room.

Her door was ajar, and peeking in I saw only Katie sound asleep on the bed.

Then I heard her voice. She spoke softly and it came from outside.

I peeked out the window.

Nila sat alone on the top step of the porch. Probably having another one of those Lev conversations she frequently had.

I grabbed my coat and stepped outside. She turned when she heard the door squeak.

"Hey," she said.

"Hey, I'm not bothering you, am I?"

"Not at all. Did you need something?" she asked.

"Just…you know…wanted to talk. Can I join you?"

"Sure."

I sat to her left on the step and nodded down to the mug in her hand. "Coffee huh? Did Ben up your intake since you're second trimester?"

"No, he doesn't know I'm drinking this. So don't tell him. Glad you have a cup, I can blame it on you."

"Your secret is safe."

"June finally down for the night?" she asked. "I heard her."

"Yeah, finally, she was tough."

"You should have given her sugar." Nila sipped her coffee.

"What?" I laughed. "Kind of counterproductive."

"No, not at all. Addy, my oldest was horrible to get to sleep. At night she would just come alive, you know. Run around. Not often, but I would just sugar her up. Yeah, she would jump off the walls for twenty minutes but bam, she was out like a light soon after."

"A sugar rush and crash."

"Yep." She nodded.

"Ben told us about the amniocentesis."

"I'm thinking about it. I mean, I know there's a chance, even slightly, that Lev was infected when the baby was conceived, but do I want to know if something is wrong or if he or she is not immune? It's not going to make a difference."

"That's true."

"What about you?" she asked. "What would you do?"

"My wife and I always turned down the extra testing because it wouldn't have made a difference. However, what is learned from it could help another mother down the road, and let's face it, this world needs to rebuild."

"It does."

"Any particular reason you're sitting in the cold?"

"Oh, it's not cold," she said. "Not yet. It will be. But this was always my favorite spot to sit. In fact, this is how me and Lev ended every night. Talking. When we were kids we'd talk on the porch like this. It was our thing."

"I wish I had gotten to know him better."

The loud, "Ha!" that was close and came from Fleck scared the hell out of me and made me actually jump. I spun around to see him sitting in a chair on the porch. "What the hell? How long have you been there?"

"The whole time."

"You didn't say anything," I told him.

"To you. Her and I were having a nice conversation."

"Oh." I nodded. "I thought you were talking to Lev again."

"Man," Fleck said. "I am surprised you bring him up or maybe not. Play that sympathy card."

Nila glanced back at him. "What the hell are you talking about, Fleck?"

"Him." Fleck pointed. "Ask Lev the next time you have one of your little talks. He's been chasing you since before Lev died. Nila, he chased you fucking here, man. Poor dude's grave is not even cold and you're wanting to take his spot."

"Oh my God," I said, shocked. "Who's even thinking about that stuff now?"

"You."

"No, I'm not. Why would you say that I'm trying to take his spot?"

"Because you're sitting in his spot for one."

I was confused, then Nila looked at me and raised her eyebrows.

"It is…was," she said.

"Oh, wow, I didn't know. It just was a good place to sit and talk."

"You could have sat on a chair," Fleck said.

"And lurk in the dark like a creeper?" I asked. "No. Why didn't you sit on the step?"

"Because he died there. Right there. That spot. He died."

Slowly I shifted my eyes to Nila.

"Yeah." She nodded. "That's true, too."

"Wow. Well, in any event, I'm not here to take his spot. If you knew me, Fleck, you'd know that."

"Then maybe we should play three things," Fleck said. "Something to do."

I asked, "What is three things?"

192

"It's a game we used to play. You think you know each other, but then you come up with three things the others would be surprised to know," Fleck explained.

"I don't know you," I replied. "So everything you say will be a surprise."

"Then you get a point for every person you surprise with something. Nila, you want to go first?"

"Nope. I want to see how it plays out first, I am very competitive."

"Is that one of your three things?" Fleck asked.

"No!" Nila answered. "It's not."

"Because you would have gotten a point," Fleck said. "I didn't know that."

"I did," I replied.

"You just can't stop with this chasing her."

After grunting, I gathered my thoughts. "Okay, I'll go first."

Fleck held out his hand. "Just list them."

"Alright. One month as a cop, I handed out five hundred and thirty-six traffic citations, the highest in New York state by one cop. I...delivered my daughter in the back seat of a car during a flood, and I play drums."

Nila stared at me. "I am surprised by two. The drum thing and citation thing because you seem so mild mannered."

Fleck laughed loudly. "The citation thing doesn't surprise me at all, he comes across as a dick. The drum thing. Because to me, you have to be cool to be a drummer."

"So that's like three points I have?" I asked.

"Yep," Fleck said. "My three things. I was held back in second grade, I met Hulk Hogan and was scared to say a word, and one foot is a half-size smaller than the other."

"Oh!" Nila blasted almost excitedly. "The shoe thing is cool. The Hulk thing shocks me because you're such an extrovert, the held back thing, nah. No surprise."

"Me, either," I added. "But the shoe and Hulk thing are. Four points. Nila."

"Alright." She took a breath. "I went to school to be a sushi chef, but I was terrible, I made more friends working at Arby's than I did my entire life, and…lately, I'm scared of everything ninety percent of the time. It's like I suddenly get weak. I put on a front, but that's what it is."

Silence.

"Wow," Fleck said. "Way to put a damper on things."

"Nila." I faced her. "You're scared because you're pregnant and you have another life to worry about. We're all here for you."

"Oh my God," Fleck blurted. "Give it a rest with the trying to tag her."

I mouthed the word, 'Tag' in question.

"You're not scared, Nila, you think you are because you don't have the big guy to lean on. Not gonna say you're the bravest person I met, because I am."

Nila snorted a laugh.

"And," Fleck added, "you suck at this game. I am not playing it with you again. Did I win?"

We all laughed. I saw through Nila though, it didn't help.

I wished she could feel like we all did. The cabin was a safe haven, and with the dead lessening outside the fence by the day, with the mutated virus out of our reach, there was nothing to be afraid of.

That, however, was something she would have to learn on her own.

TWENTY-ONE

YOU'LL SEE

Nila
October 5

There was a sense of normalcy that returned to our daily living at the cabin. As each day passed my paranoia decreased. I was superstitious. If I broke a mirror I fretted over it for a day about having seven years' bad luck. God forbid a bird flew in the house, I was on edge for days about who was going to die.

Once when I was younger and married to Paul I had gone to a psychic party. Girlfriends from work, which happened to be a supermarket at the time, gathered for crackers, cheese, and other foods while we all took turns waiting to see the psychic.

Paul hated the idea I was going to go, not only because it cost fifty dollars, but he knew the way I was.

He said the people at work told him the psychics all implied the same thing. He even made me a list. Cheating spouse, job change, someone I knew would be having a baby. He was right, she did say all that, but I found a way to make each prediction seem as if it came true.

When Katie started doing her strange drawings and then spitting out things that happened to already be true or came true, suddenly the suspicious side of me disappeared and I went into denial.

Because other than knowing I was pregnant, most of her predictions were horrible.

Why couldn't my child predict positive things?

She'd eerily placed everyone's name on a vial. It was disturbing, something that made me feel as if she condemned them to a fate.

More than I wanted to admit, that stayed with me. I was absolutely insane about it. Other than Fleck's depiction of eating Ben, no one really knew about those vials, except Ben.

It pushed me to the brink.

Ben kept telling me it was a set up by The Colony. Trying to get us to join them.

He insisted a lot of Katie's comments about things she didn't know could be easily explained away.

She gave me a cracker, not because she knew I was pregnant, but because after the head injury they were they only thing I could eat. Ben kept feeding them to me.

I may not have known Fleck's real last name, but Ben did. Another thing Katie could have known.

And the fact that The Colony was invading us that day? Katie brought them to us.

He dismissed it all.

Her drawings garnished attention. The worse they were they more attention they got.

Was she twisted?

Absolutely. But she was growing up in a world where the walking dead ruled.

The Colony used Katie to scare us.

After two weeks, I believed that.

A part of me truly believed that the day they knocked us out they had infected us. How convenient it was for it to be a tradeoff, the cure for us to live there.

Almada had one of those scanners in her desk, she probably had Katie write the names on the tubes.

After ten days with no one showing any signs of infection, I started to relax.

No one had a single symptom. Everyone was healthy with the exception of the slight cold Bella developed. I scanned her twice a day, and checked her temperature.

It was just a cold, easily explained. She never left the camp. She went with me and Fleck to get winter coats, and we got caught in the rain.

End of story.

Each day that passed, the prospect of having to live in The Colony grew slim.

Almada didn't even mention it when Katie and I returned for her weekly check-up. In fact, Almada and I had a chuckle about Katie's morbid predictions.

I also decided to go forth with the amniocentesis. It seemed my belly grew more each day, and when I felt the first flutter of life, so came the true concern about my unborn child.

Bad weather delayed the doctor from Minnesota, but I was glad to hear he would be there when I brought Katie for her weekly blood work.

I was nervous, and surprised that everyone wanted to go because they were going to do an ultrasound as well.

Even Fleck wanted to be there.

The baby became a new sense of excitement for us all, and in turn, I got excited.

"If you have a boy," Fleck said, "just don't name him Lev."

That was horrible. I loved Lev's name and I hoped I did have a son so I could call him Little Lev.

The day had come and we drew straws. Sean won. Fleck said he cheated.

Ben told me to get whatever I needed done, because he was putting me on twenty-four-hour bed rest after the procedure.

Katie wanted to be in the ultrasound room, but since I worried something could be wrong, I didn't want her there if it was.

When we arrived at The Colony, I could tell Sean was nervous. Maybe scared he'd get detained, but it was the opposite. Some of the men there knew him and were happy to see him.

They had made a lot of progress in a week with transforming the high school to a medical facility. After they took Katie, they brought me to the room where I would get the procedure done.

Undressed from the waist down and on the table, I increasingly grew nervous. I breathed out slowly through my parted lips as my heart raced out of control.

The ultrasound machine and screen were to my left and made it so real.

I was having another child.

What kind of life would he or she have? Was it fair? Then again, there was nothing I could do about it.

"It's gonna be fine," Sean said as he sat next to me.

"I know. Just nervous."

"Me, too," he said.

"I never had one of these done."

"Ultrasound or amnio?"

"Amnio," I said.

"Me either."

That made me laugh and I felt the lump in my chest when there was a knock on the door.

"Nila Carter?" He poked his head in. "I'm Doctor Rosen." He entered with an extended hand. "Nice to meet you."

I shook his hand. He seemed pleasant and friendly. He looked more like a scientist than a baby doctor. Mostly bald. He wasn't a tall man at all. He was thin, and he wore glasses and a white jacket over his blue scrubs.

He then shook Sean's hand. "And you are?"

"Sean."

"Father?"

"No," Sean said. "Friend."

"The father passed away," I told him. "Which is one of the reasons I'm doing this. He died of the virus."

"I see, well, as far as answers for fetal abnormalities and so forth, you won't get answers today, but I promise in a couple days you'll have them. However, Dr. Hillgrove assured me that as far as fetal immunity, we'll know before you leave. We're not backed up in the lab like the old days." He winked, then a knock at the door drew his attention.

The door opened and a middle-aged woman walked in. She pushed a tray that was covered and handed him a chart. "Hi, Nila, congratulations on the baby. We're excited. We don't see many pregnancies." She immediately walked to the machine and made sure it was on and working.

199

"Three in our colony," Dr. Rosen said. "We travel to others when needed. Still not a lot."

"How was your trip in?" I asked, making small talk.

"Good. We arrived yesterday," he said.

"You work as a team?" I asked.

Rosen smiled. "For twenty-two years. She's my wife. Now…relax, okay?"

I nodded.

"I know you're concerned, but I can assure you that baby inside is fine and protected by your immunities no matter what the results. So let's get started. Date of your last menstrual cycle?"

"I don't know. I kind of stopped getting them regularly," I replied. "But I know when it happened and from that we estimate I'm seventeen weeks."

He lifted my shirt and exposed my belly, keeping me covered from the hips down. He pulled out a tape and measured me. A procedure I knew well. "You said seventeen weeks?"

"Yes."

"You're measuring about twenty-two weeks. Feeling any life?"

"Yes, I just started."

"Good. We're going to do a quick ultrasound for placement first," he explained. "Gwen?" he spoke to his wife.

She squirted the thick gel-like fluid on my belly and handed him the wand. "Can you see the screen?"

It was a slight strain on my neck, but I could.

The second he put the wand on my belly, I heard the heartbeat. That made me grin. I couldn't really see anything, it looked like bad reception, but I could tell he did. I was smiling until he immediately pulled the wand from me.

I watched the look on his face as he made eye contact with his wife. "Go ahead. Get another."

Gwen tapped my leg as she walked by me and left the room.

"What is it? What's wrong?" I asked.

"The procedure will take a little longer," he explained. "There's two of them in there."

"What? Two?" I asked in shock.

Sean laughed. "Twins?"

"Yep."

"Fucking Lev," I said in shock. "Two?"

"Two. Now...let's take a look at them." He placed the wand to my stomach again.

While the actual amniocentesis didn't take long it was unnerving and painful. Rosen tried to be as gentle as he could. But I could feel my stomach cramping up and the burning as he placed the long needle into my belly.

At one point I actually held Sean's hand, squeezing it to transfer pain.

I kept thinking of Lev and how happy he'd be to find out it wasn't just one baby, but two.

Then I grew sad that he was going to miss it.

The first amniocentesis was the hardest. I didn't know what to expect. The second was easier, he said there was slightly more fluid in that sac.

He told me they were definitely fraternal and not identical because there were two placentas and two sacs. He also said I could stop blaming Lev because it was all on me for popping out two eggs.

201

When he was finished he handed the final tube to Gwen and she promptly took them from the room.

"One hour." He brought the covers over me. "You don't move for one hour, you hear? Let us know if there's any cramping or bleeding. We'll let you go, but you go home and rest."

"A doctor lives with us," I said. "He already mentioned that."

"I'm sure he'll also mention to you that twins come early. Dr. Hillgrove told me you don't live in Colony Alpha. Is there a reason for that?"

"I love where we live. It is my father's cabin and it's been part of me all my life," I replied.

"I can understand that, but they can come early. If they're premature, you won't have the means to care for them in the cabin. We can have everything ready here."

"I know. I mean I didn't think of that because I thought there was only one. But we're only an hour away, and first sign of pains, I can come here."

Rosen nodded. "Labor can be stopped if it's too early, but if you take too long to get here…you know what…you think about it."

"What are you suggesting?" Sean asked.

"I'm suggesting that she thinks about staying at The Colony until the babies are born. And I'll leave you two to talk. Think about it, Nila. Now give us some time, and we can at least set your mind at ease about the virus. Push the button if you need anything."

"Dr. Rosen," I called to him as he opened the door. "Did you by chance see the sex?"

"I did." He smiled and then walked out.

"Oh man." Sean stood. "Talk about a cliff hanger." He walked over to the ultrasound table and lifted the small, printed sheet of squares. "She made you pictures. Two, Nila, two. And I got to hear it first." When he noticed I wasn't looking, he tapped me on the arm. "What's up? I thought you'd stare at these forever. I am."

"Do you think he said that because Almada wants us to live here so bad?"

"Almada wants Katie to live here. Be the girl in the plastic bubble."

"What do you think about that?"

"Keeping Katie here?"

I nodded.

"I mean, I understand their reasons. Come on, you remember my mindset. When I first met you I was all about The Colony and wanted you guys to stay. Let's face it, Nila, Katie is the key and they want to make sure nothing happens to her."

"But you don't feel that way about The Colony now?"

"I got soured," he replied. "Watching it fall when they weren't ready. Colony One got too big. Too many people and not enough soldiers to protect it. In hindsight it was a disaster waiting to happen."

"I don't want to live here, Sean."

"Neither do I. And we can protect Katie. We can protect her at the cabin as well as they can protect her here."

I reached up for the strip of ultrasound pictures and took them. I stared in disbelief at the pictures marked Baby A and Baby B. "What about them?"

"We can protect the babies. Are you worried about if they come early?"

"Yeah, I am. I know twins come early."

"And I had a cousin who was two weeks late with twins," Sean said. "Listen. It's twenty-five miles from the cabin to here. Top speed we can make it in forty, maybe even less. That's plenty of time. Think about it. Before all this shit happened, how long did most people have to travel to get to a hospital? Twenty or thirty minutes. It's not that long and not that far."

"And we know you can deliver a baby in a car."

Sean laughed. "Yeah, about that. I kind of um…I lied about that to see what Fleck would say. Him and his damn game."

I reached up giving him a playful smack to his arm.

"It'll work out, Nila. Talk to Ben. See what he says. I don't think we will have to live here."

"We?" I asked. "I don't expect any of you to live here with us."

"The way we fought over who was going to come to the ultrasound I don't think you'll be far from any of us when it gets close to baby time."

"Man," I breathed out the word with my exhale. "Almada goes to any extremes to get my daughter to live here."

It wasn't long after that Katie came barreling in the room announcing she was done for the day.

"I made four more doses, Mommy," she said brightly.

"Four? I thought they got six."

"Almie said they needed some to copy. I don't know what that means."

"They're trying to make enough to save the world."

Katie climbed on a chair next to me. "I don't think that will ever happen."

204

I raised my eyes to Sean.

"Hey, Katie." He touched her head and spoke gently. "How about you trying to say positive things for the next couple days? Nothing bad, no pictures of Fleck being a deader."

"But what if it wants to come out?" she asked.

"How about this? When you want to say something bad, like when it comes to you," Sean explained. "When that happens, think of something good."

"But what if it's really bad?" Katie asked.

"Then you ask yourself if it is something that can be changed. If you think it can be changed by saying something, then say it. But…word it nicely."

I decided to explain. "For example, instead of drawing Fleck as a deader, you could have um…drawn him lying in bed holding his tummy. It would have said he was going to get sick."

"It would not be as fun to draw, Mommy," she said. "But I'll try. I will not say the bad things that come to my mind. And if I do, I will try to say them nicely."

"Good girl. Now…" I handed her the ultrasound pictures. "What do you see?"

She looked at them.

My stomach started to flutter, wondering if my precocious child was holding back bad.

"Why does it say Baby A and Baby B on this one?"

"Because there's two," I explained. "Two babies in my belly, not one."

"Oh! Mommy! I'm gonna have two brothers?" She quickly covered her mouth. "Sorry, I didn't mean to say the bad. But I said it nicely."

"Katie." I chuckled. "Brothers aren't a bad thing."

"You don't think?" She cringed and shook her head. "Boys smell."

"Well, we don't know if they're boys," I said. "We have to wait and find out."

After saying those words, it dawned on me we were still waiting on those results and another wave of nervousness came over me.

Katie spun in her chair. "Oh. Maybe Almie knows. She's coming now."

After a curious look exchange with Sean, I asked Katie, "How do you know?"

"You can hear her heels clicking."

I shivered out a breath. Once again, I was too concerned about my daughter's gift of knowledge, if indeed she had it.

There was a knock on the door, and sure enough Almada walked in with Dr. Rosen.

"We have results," Dr. Rosen said with heavy exhale.

I knew by the look on his face something was wrong. Almada was there and that made me slightly distrustful of what was going to be said.

"Two babies," Rosen stated, looking down at the chart. "Two different results."

"Baby B," said Almada, "is immune. What level of immunity at this time we cannot tell, but we know Baby B has at least your immunities, Nila. Baby A, however…"

"Is not immune?" I asked.

"No. It's strange." Almada glanced at Rosen. "We can't explain it. Of course, we're going to run the test again. We have to."

"It makes zero sense to me." Rosen looked down, then at me. "By the readouts Dr. Hillgrove and her team got. Baby A...is already infected."

"Wait, what?" I asked, shocked. "How is that possible?"

Rosen lifted his hands in a symbol of defeat. "It's not. All logic and science is out the window here. I don't know. I honestly don't. Yes, there have been cases in the past where the fetus can get a virus from the mother. But that's when the mother is infected and passes it."

"Which makes this an anomaly," said Almada. "Because your blood resists the virus."

It was a good thing I wasn't standing, because the news would have knocked me over. "What does this mean for the other baby?"

"Baby B is immune," Almada explained.

"So Baby A," I said. "Will die?"

Katie gasped loudly. "No! No, he won't die! Mommy, we aren't saying bad things."

"I hate this term," Almada stated. "But we don't know. We can try to inject the serum into the fluid or the cord. Which may or may not work."

"That's not something I would recommend," Rosen said. "Simply because it takes a skilled expert in fetal surgery, which I am not. How the baby and when the baby was infected is hard to tell. We do know that no living being survives the virus after ten days."

"Meaning, the baby will die inside of me," I said sadly.

Rosen nodded. "All we can do is simply monitor the pregnancy and go from there."

Sean spoke up. "Is it possible, just hear me out, I'm not an expert. Is it possible that the baby has the virus, but is not sick? Like…like a carrier?"

Almada nodded. "That is actually a possibility. If the child survives the next week and a half, I think that is the situation we are looking at."

"Unfortunately," Rosen added, "because of the pregnancy being high risk with twins, I won't do another amnio for at least six weeks, but we'll get a very good idea then."

"Three D imaging," Almada said. "We can search it out, and in a few weeks we can see features that will tell us more."

I stifled a breath. "If the baby lives?"

"Mommy." Katie grabbed my hand. "He will live."

Of all the things my daughter had said over the past year, that was one thing I hoped was an accurate prediction.

"Nila," Almada said gently. "I know how adamant you are about not living here. But please think about it now."

I nodded.

"Almie, we'll be back," Katie said. "Mommy will have to pack my things. But we'll be back to get…" She stopped talking and looked at me. She bit her bottom lip, then smiled after a few second. "We'll be back to get…all the help we need for my baby brothers."

I knew that wasn't what she was going to say. Yes, I told Almada I would think about it, but I wasn't. I didn't need to. One of my babies was infected and there was nothing that could be done.

What I needed was to go back to the cabin and talk to Ben. It wasn't his specialty, but I trusted his advice.

I got dressed and thanked Dr. Rosen who said he would see me in a week when I brought Katie back.

Finding out I was carrying twins and then the chance of one not surviving was overwhelming and a lot to process. I felt numb.

Sean asked the stock question as we got into the truck. "Are you okay?"

"I will be. I just need to think this through." I buckled Katie's seat and got into the truck. "You know it's strange. Now I may have to rely on The Colony's help when all I wanted to do was live my life at the cabin."

"You can still live at the cabin." Sean started the truck. "It's not a far drive."

"I know, but now they have something else, other than the six vials of cure they dangled like a carrot to lure us."

"Gotta need the cure to be lured," Sean replied.

"Oh!" Katie said brightly from the back seat. "Bella doesn't need the cure anymore. Is that positive, Mommy?"

"Yes, baby it is." I looked back at her with a smile. "I'm proud of you."

We hit the road and headed home. Not only did I face lots of decisions ahead of me, I faced the daunting task of how to explain it to everyone else.

The moment I saw the expression on Ben's face, I felt a sense of relief. I told him about the twins and about what the tests said.

"This is fantastic." Ben stared at the pictures. "Two of them. Oh, boy, things are gonna get interesting around here."

"Like I said before." Fleck peeked at the pictures. "Kid Mountain, and this one looks like Lev."

"Ben? Did you hear what I said?" I asked. "About Baby A having the virus."

"It's preposterous," Ben replied. "They're either lying to you or they are missing the boat on something pretty interesting. A baby in utero cannot catch an airborne virus from a mother who is not infected. A mother who has immunities. It's like saying a kid gets chicken pox in the womb when the mother can't get it. Impossible." He handed back the picture strip. "If indeed the test showed he or she has the virus, they aren't infected. The baby isn't going to get sick and die in utero. It's part of his genetics, and that high and mighty Hillgrove lady is not thinking about what possibilities that can bring."

Fleck shook his head. "A kid genetically carrying the virus. Where's the positive? No offense, Nila."

"None taken."

"I don't know," Ben said. "It's not for me to figure out. I do know this. You shouldn't worry. I'm not worried. And as far as having twins and going into early labor, we're close to Colony One should we need neonatal care. It's not far and if you have early contractions that need to be stopped, I'll give you a couple shots of that grain alcohol of Lisa's—it's the same thing as the magnesium sulfate used at hospitals."

"Thank you, Ben." I leaned in and kissed him on the cheek then stared down to the strip of ultrasound photos. "I'm gonna go show Bella, she'll get a kick out of these. Where is she?"

"She and Christian took a nap in the RV," Ben said. "I think they're up though, I heard Christian crying. But, Nila, back here and bed rest. Okay?"

210

"Okay, promise." I turned around and Sean was standing there.

"See?" he asked. "I told you."

"You did. I'll be back." I reached for the door, paused, and looked to Katie. "Did you want to come with me, Sweetie?"

"No, Mommy."

"Okay." I shrugged and headed out the door.

As soon as I stepped out, I heard Christian crying. Bella worked so hard to be a mom to him, I knew it exhausted her. Maybe she was still sleeping.

I knocked on the RV and opened the door. "Bella?" I called out and stepped in. "Hey, I have something to show you."

She didn't reply.

"Bella?" I stepped further in, and I could see her in the rear room, her bedroom. She was on her knees reached for something by the closet, her back to me. "Hey," I called again, walking toward her. "Is Chris alright? Did you lose him?" I joked. "My kids used to hide and get stuck all the…"

Then with a sharp, rigid movement she turned her head and faced me.

Her mouth was red with blood, her face pale and her eyes had lost their color.

"Shit." I reached back for my piece, drew it forward. The safety was on and I had popped one in the chamber when I checked my weapon at The Colony.

At that second she jumped to her feet, spun completely around, and raged my way with a snarling scream.

I didn't want to do it. I swore as my hands actually shook for the first time.

Safety off, I racked the slide, gripped the gun, and just as she was on me, I fired.

TWENTY-TWO

NEVER CLOSE ENOUGH

Sean

Bang!

We all heard the shot. After the initial shock of it, all of us turned wide-eyed to the sound, then Fleck, Ben, and I raced out.

I was the last out of the door telling Katie, "Stay here with June," before shutting it and running to the RV.

Fleck was already inside the RV, with Ben making his way through the door.

I could hear Nila inside. "Christian. Christian baby, where are you, come out?"

The baby cried.

"Follow the blood," Fleck said.

I made it inside.

Bella lay twisted on the floor of the RV's kitchen area, a clear gunshot to the head. Ben crouched over her.

He peered up at me. "She was sick and turned."

"How…how did we not know?" I asked.

Ben shook his head. "I don't know."

It was hard to concentrate, hard to think. Nila beckoned Christian while he cried.

"Nila, he won't come out. He's bleeding," Fleck said.

I glanced to the rear room, I could see both Nila and Fleck on the floor and I raced back.

"Let me try." Nila inched Fleck over and crawled on the floor. "Got him. Ben!" she shouted.

What was going on? I couldn't see. Ben blasted by me to the back room. He started barking orders, "get me this, get me that, get my bag."

Fleck flew by me out the door. I felt helpless just standing there and more so when I saw Ben carry the little boy who just had his first birthday.

Christian kicked and cried. I could see the blood on him, but didn't know where the injury was until Ben placed him on the kitchen table.

Nila handed him a towel, and when Ben brought it down to Christian I saw the bite mark on the side of his belly.

"Jesus," I said.

"We have to get him to The Colony," Nila said, rushed. "We have to get him there. We need to get him the serum."

Ben looked at Nila. "Do you think the serum works on the bite strain?"

"We have to try, right."

"Is there enough time?" I asked. "Will he make it there?"

Ben checked the wound. "It's bad, but The Colony isn't that far. Nila, get me a blanket. Sean, get the car ready, we'll radio them on the way there. And have Fleck keep trying after we go."

Fleck returned right after Ben had said that. "Why am I staying behind?"

"Because Sean knows how to get there and get us in, I need to take care of Christian in the back," Ben replied.

"And Nila?" Fleck asked.

"She has to make sure we get that serum." He accepted the blanket Nila handed him. "Whatever it takes to get it."

There was a rush of static before Fleck's voice came over the radio. "It's me. I got through."

I looked in the rearview mirror as Nila lifted the radio. "Thank God," she replied. "What did they say? We tried to reach them."

"They said they'll meet you at the receiving center with the serum," Fleck replied.

"Did they say if it works on a bite?" she asked.

"They didn't know. How is he?"

"He stopped crying, but he's moving. Ben's working on him."

"Keep me posted."

"I will, and thanks." She set down the radio and gave her attention back to Christian.

My view of what was happening was restricted to what I could see in the rearview mirror. We had taken Betsy; it had a roomier back seat plus she moved pretty well down the highway.

Ben was on the floor of the back seat. Christian's legs were wrapped tight in a blanket to keep him from moving. His head rested on Nila's lap while Ben sutured his wound. It seemed to stop bleeding. I didn't know a child could lose so much blood.

What was happening was heartbreaking. I didn't know Bella and Christian as long as the others, I could only imagine the pain they were going through.

Bella had a cold, a simple cold. I was with Nila when she checked her in the morning. How did she turn so fast? Did

215

we miss something? One of the outward symptoms, we had to.

And Christian. He was just a baby, a little boy who trusted Bella. How scared he must have been. He didn't know what was happening, only that he was in pain and Bella, somebody who loved and took care of him, had caused it.

The children of the world were the greatest tragedies.

Every movie or book I read glosses over the tragedy of the children.

It was one of the most ungodly painful things to think about. It didn't have to be your child, just any child. Thinking of what they endured and being so helpless to do anything about it or much less understand.

I tried to drive fast, but I had to drive cautiously. It was a delicate procedure and one swerve, one hard stop could do more harm than good.

"How is he?" I asked. "Why isn't he crying?"

Nila answered, "I think he just passed out. His fingers are still holding mine."

"Almost finished," Ben announced. "How far are we?"

"Another twenty minutes. Ten miles from eighty-one." My eyes shifted from mirror to road.

"That's good," Ben said. "We'll be in there soon then. I'm finished."

Another shift upward of my eyes and I saw Ben snipped the suture.

"They may want to redo this," Ben said. "But we got the bleeding to stop."

I felt somewhat relieved and hopeful. The Colony wasn't far, they did have a cure, we didn't know if it worked on an infection caused by a bite. But they were going to try. We had to fight for Christian's life.

I felt better, hopeful, then something seeped through in Nila's voiced that erased all that.

A simple calling of Ben's name; it had a weakness, a quiver. "Ben."

I glanced to the mirror to see Nila had sat up.

"Ben, something's wrong. He stopped holding my hand." Then her voice turned to panic and ladened with the sound of agonizing sadness. "Oh, God, Ben. Ben, he's gone."

The way she cried and sobbed the words, I knew Nila felt the life pass from the child.

"No, no, no," Ben grunted. "This isn't happening. It won't happen."

"Should I pull over?" I asked.

"Keep going," Ben beckoned.

I hit the gas harder, but kept looking up. Telling myself to drive, just drive, torn between that and having to see what was going on.

I saw Ben slide Christian from Nila's lap to lay him flat on the back seat. He began CPR. He'd do compressions, then the breath, pause and listen.

He kept doing it steadily.

It went on for five good minutes, we had made it to Interstate eighty-one.

Ben did not give up. With every compression, he begged the baby to come back, please come back.

He got what he asked for, but not the way he wanted it.

The gurgling and cat-like cry rang out, and I knew it was Christian, but not the boy we all loved.

Ben grunted loudly, as the snarls continued and Nila cried out once.

I couldn't see and I pressed my foot to the brake. The vibration and shaking of the car told me there was a struggle and at eighty miles an hour it took a while for the car to come to a stop.

After throwing the car in park, I opened the door, ran to the back driver's side and flung open the door.

Ben sat up, leaning nearly to the other car door, fighting with a twenty-four-pound child. Nila struggled to pull him from Ben. Christian's body wriggled, legs kicking. His arms flailed violently striking down hard on Ben's head. Sounds of a mad young animal screaming out were steady and loud despite his mouth being locked onto Ben's ear.

Blood poured down Ben's chest. I reached in, grabbing on to Christian's torso. I wanted to pull harder, but he had such a grip on Ben's ear, I was afraid he'd rip it off.

The noise level was out of control in the confined space of the back seat. Christian crying out, Ben struggling. It was devastating, chaotic, building and building in insanity. Trying to stop a small toddler from their maddening rage seemed impossible.

Then…silence.

I held on to Christian's ribcage and I felt him go limp. With an inward arch of his spine, he fell backwards, releasing Ben's ear, and his arms dropped lifeless over my hands.

I breathed heavily and looked down to his head which was pressed near to my chest.

I don't know what I thought in those after seconds. Perhaps the virus hit children differently and they died quickly. I looked at Ben who held his ear, blood pouring from it, the child's legs still on Ben's chest, and when I turned my head toward Nila, I realized what had happened, what caused the situation to abruptly halt.

Breathing heavily, with an absolute mortified look on her face, Nila stared down to the knife she held in her hand.

Her hands shook. With wide eyes she looked down. I saw it on her face, and by her actions I could tell the knife was repulsive to her, as if it had made her do it. She tossed it down with a short, gut sounding scream. Hurriedly, she grabbed for the door handle, her bloody fingers slipping several times on it before she finally managed to open it. Nearly rolling out, she stumbled from the car.

I placed Christian down on the seat and jumped out of the car as well.

Racing around the back of the car, I saw Nila. She paced back and forth in small, agitated circles, her hands over her face.

"Nila, are you hurt?" I asked. "Bit? Scratched?"

The word "No" was muddled from behind her hands.

"Nila…"

She unleashed a chesty and sobbing, "Oh God, what did I do? Oh my God, what did I do? I'm sorry. I'm sorry, I'm so sorry."

"Nila, you did what had to be done."

She lowered her hands, mouth tense, she shook her head quickly, then as she stepped back, I watched her legs weaken. It wasn't illness that caused her to stumble, it was emotions. Every inch of her body and soul was submerged in a guilty sorrow she couldn't contain.

The second I reached to steady her, she fell into my arms and broke down.

I struggled to keep her standing when she wanted to collapse. She cried out of control. It was as if everything horrible and devastating she had experienced came out in that roadside moment.

It scared me. I had never seen her or anyone react like that.

There were no words I could give; anything that came from my mouth would have been useless.

Holding her, I saw Ben slowly stagger toward us. He held the blanket to his ear.

"Nila, we need to go," Ben said. "We need to go now. I…feel it, Nila, this thing is fast. It's coursing through my veins, I can feel it."

Nila slowly pulled from my embrace. She looked at Ben and I saw the instant transformation in her. Suddenly she knew it wasn't about her pain, guilt, or loss. It wasn't even about Christian anymore, it was about Ben.

And without any more words being said or any delays, the two of them loaded into the front bench seat of old Betsy.

I closed both back doors, got back in the driver's seat, and at an even faster speed headed to The Colony.

Dr. Hillgrove was waiting at the receiving center with a surgical team, and the serum. Expecting Christian, but getting Ben. She didn't ask any questions about the toddler, she just injected Ben right away and they took him to a med room they had set up and waiting.

Nila and I were a different story. They checked us for bites and scratches despite both of us insisting we didn't have any wounds.

Nila was a mess, it was a horrible strong front she put on. Her face was pale, it was obvious she had been through an emotional ordeal. We all had, but Nila had taken on quite a bit with Bella and Christian.

"Will you let Dr. Rosen have a look at you?" Almada asked. "You did have that amnio not long ago. I will assume you just went through a terrifying situation."

Nila nodded. "Yeah, yeah, I think…I think that would be a good idea. 'Cause I think, no, I'm pretty sure I'm bleeding."

I was confused by that, and before I could comment I thought she wasn't bit or scratched, I realized what she meant.

The whooshing fetal heartbeat was steady and strong through the small speaker of the diagnostic machine. It sounded great to me, but what did I know. Dr. Rosen let the sounds of the heartbeat play and then turned it down.

He said nothing, his eyes peering to the screen of the ultrasound while he moved the wand on Nila's stomach.

I wanted to reach out to Fleck for several reasons. Tell him everything that had happened and make sure they were all okay. But it had been nonstop since we arrived at The Colony—a day's worth of rushing in just the two hours we were there.

Rosen's exam seemed to take forever. Once we got to the medical facility, he checked Nila without me in the room, then brought me in for the ultrasound.

It was quiet, so quiet.

"Okay." He turned off the machine. "Everything looks good."

I was holding my breath, I could only imagine how Nila felt.

Rosen continued, "Placenta is fine. I'm not seeing anything. Both babies look great. No subchorionic hematoma. When I examined you, the cervix was tight. Are you having any cramping, tightening?"

Nila shook her head. "None."

"Good, then I'm going to go with my original diagnosis. The stress of what happened, along with the amniocentesis caused the bleeding. There's no other reason that I'm seeing. It should subside by tonight."

"Thank you."

I saw Rosen getting ready to say something else when Almada knocked on the door, then stepped in.

"How is she?" Almada asked.

"Good," Rosen answered.

I asked, "How's Ben?"

"He's out of surgery and doing well," Almada replied. "He's in recovery. We won't know until the twenty-four-hour mark if the serum worked, but I'm confident."

"You told Fleck," Nila said, "that you weren't sure it would work."

"That's because the patient was a baby with a life-threatening wound. Ben is neither," Almada said. "However, Nila, with Bella…with the young woman dying of the virus. It's there. It's in your camp."

"I know."

"We need to get the serum to Fleck and the two children as soon as possible. It belongs to your family."

"Yeah." Nila nodded again. "I remember the deal."

"Nila." Almada stepped closer. "I'm not going to blackmail you and Katie to live here to save the life of those in the cabin. That is your choice. Today should have been enough to show you that you need to be near here. Katie needs to be protected until we can replicate what her body makes."

"Until then," I spoke up, "I mean until a decision is made, can we get the serum to them or should we bring them here?"

"I'd like to bring them here," Almada answered. "I need to test to make sure it works for them."

Nila sat up. "Okay, we'll go back and…"

"Whoa. Whoa." Rosen stopped her. "You're not going anywhere. I mean that. I'm having them prep you a room on the floor. You need bed rest and need to take it easy for two weeks. I'm firm on that."

"You know Ben would say the same thing," I told her. "Why don't I go back to the cabin, get Fleck and the kids?"

"In that car?" Nila asked.

"I'll drive it back and we'll bring the wagon." I faced Almada. "How long will you need them here for testing?"

"Ten days. I'll find them a place to stay so they're comfortable. All of you," she said. "If you don't mind, I'd like to go with you. It would be a lot easier with me to explain what is going on to everyone."

"Can we take that sweet black SUV?" I asked.

"Of course, I'll go get things situated."

Almada conveyed her well wishes to Nila and left, telling me she'd meet me in the lobby. Not long after she left, Dr. Rosen gave a firm, "Stay in bed" to Nila then went to set her up with a room and was going to send a nurse in with a sedative.

Nila didn't argue that.

I waited until the nurse came.

"Fleck knows where the keys are," Nila told me. "Make sure you lock up."

"I will, and I'll go back to the cabin every couple days to check while we're here. I'll be back."

I knew it wouldn't be long until the sedative kicked in and I wanted to leave her be.

Nila not only had decisions to make, she had a lot on her mind. I knew she was struggling with the fact she'd had to make the decision to put Christian to rest.

Struggling was putting it mildly, she was in utter turmoil. Nila had killed infected and deaders, she had killed marauders.

This was different.

The mother in her had to have been blinded. I don't even think she saw him as a monster, but just a child. It didn't matter what he did, how he acted, he was still a baby. One she'd watched come into the world.

Making it even worse for her.

She needed to rest and to not think about what had transpired. I had a feeling it would be a long time, if ever, before she stopped thinking of the events of this day.

TWENTY-THREE

UNTIL ONE DAY

Nila
October 22

The cabin looked cold. No smoke emerged from the chimney, the shutters were closed, and the windows were frosted on the outside from the drop in temperature. It was the first time I had been back in weeks.

Sean kept his word, he'd been back, to check, and secure it.

"How does it feel?" Ben asked me.

"Strange, and I know it wasn't that long."

"You're looking at it differently."

"I guess."

I jingled the keys and unlocked the door as Ben went back to the truck.

Stepping inside felt strange, but right.

It was cold in there, but there was nothing the winter would ruin.

There were many times in my life my father closed it up for the winter. Not always, but there were times he had to.

I was back.

The very first morning after my two-week bed rest I wanted to go out salvaging. I needed to do it, it was almost an addiction.

Dr. Rosen and Ben both said it wasn't a good idea. Not yet. A few more weeks and he'd feel better about me doing things.

I had to, for the sake of my children, the ones unborn and for Katie to focus on the future.

Ben had recovered fully, although Almada worried it wasn't going to work. It took several days for the virus to decrease in his blood stream.

When Almada and Sean went back to the cabin, she scanned Fleck. He had the virus.

Sawyer did not. Neither did June. It was a huge relief for Sean when he found out she was immune. Not the extent that Katie was, but she was like me and him.

The entire time I was hospitalized, I blamed myself for Christian's death.

Because Bella turned so rapidly, the serum would not have worked even if we caught it a day earlier.

Upon the post-mortem exam, Almada discovered the veins were black around her ankle and Bella never said anything. She had it for about four days, the same amount of time she had that cold. But I scanned her, I scanned her religiously.

It was a lesson in science. The young didn't need a cure as much they needed a vaccine, and the serum was not that, not yet. Not that the serum wouldn't work, but it had to be delivered quickly.

Bella's death was not completely in vain. It taught Almada that the youth showed it differently and reacted differently.

She had lumped them all together, old, young. When it wasn't at all that way.

It was a long road ahead for us. The young were the only way the human race would survive and not go extinct, but they were dying off exponentially.

This would be the next step, saving the young.

Do all they could to preserve life. All the Colonies were working on a mission, a wide-spread plan to gather the children, as many as they could find.

With the virus slowing in the cold, at least in the northeast, they had time to make a plan, a way to keep the young, house them, protect them not only from the deaders, but from the invisible force that threatened our existence.

It was out there.

The Colony had made great strides in curing it, but until they replicated what Katie's antibodies did, the serum was like gold.

Hence another reason to protect Katie at all costs. Not just from the dead, but from the living as well.

When I first heard of the plan to gather every baby, child, and teenager they could and secure them, admittedly it scared me. Would it be a prison they could never leave?

Would they ever know the freedom of doing what they wanted, when they wanted?

To live and to survive as a species…there had to be change.

Change was inevitable across the board, whether we liked it or not. People changed, places changed.

I always believed people modified the way they behaved, their habits. That was what changed, not the core of who a person was. It is in us from our youth, we are bad or good, strong or weak, indifferent or caring.

We had the ability to adjust.

I had to adjust. I saw that coming.

I never thought of myself as a strong woman, but I was awesome at putting on a front. Relying on others to keep me brave. The habit of doing things that made me look invincible got better as I got older, and especially after the world took a nosedive. In my youth, for some reason, I began to feel indifferent about things, never showing over the top emotions.

Again, until the world turned into a wasteland.

Lev would argue that he one hundred percent believed people could change and would point to me as an example. The Nila he knew would have never poisoned a well killing dozens of people without batting an eye.

The world changed me, he said.

Not true.

The world just magnified who I was

I never really had huge compassion for people outside my circle and that carried over and was even made worse into the apocalypse.

I cared deeply for those I let in. I hated and was crushed that not only did I have to end Bella's and Christian's lives, but the blow that it took to do so, I did instinctively and without thought.

The thought came after.

The only difference was those I relied on for strength had dwindled to nearly nil.

My father, brother, stepmother...Lev.

All gone.

Each day that passed, the strength they gave me slipped further away.

Losing Lev was the final blow. It took a few months, but I saw myself crumbling.

Every day, a bit of me left…slowly I felt like I was one of the dead. Walking mindlessly, acting without thought, just moving forward.

Lev had been in my life since he was ten. When he was the oversized boy who didn't speak a word of English. Funny how I was his protector back then from the bullies and what life in his new, strange, adopted world brought him.

But as we grew older the rules flipped.

When the virus came and the deaders took over, Lev was my iron curtain.

It didn't matter if I pulled the trigger or him, I attributed it to him making me strong.

I believed that, and I feared when he died I would no longer be strong.

The final blow to what remained of my strength, at least I believed, was my decision to stay at Colony Alpha.

It was a build up to my surrender.

After all that we had been through, staying in The Colony was cowering in a corner.

But was it?

I struggled with the decision.

The scientific community needed access to my daughter and the few of us that were immune. We weren't the future, we were the key to their being a future.

The Colony wasn't some futuristic, strong arm, totalitarian society, as asinine as they behaved, they were truly trying to save mankind.

Did Almada want to work seven days a week, every hour she was awake? I would wager she would rather be on a beach or in a cabin somewhere, but she knew her responsibility.

We all had a responsibility to each other, not just ourselves, and the moment the world turned to a 'me first' place, we were finished.

Despite all that happened we weren't there yet.

And like it or not, I had to admit, I was first in the 'me first' mentality movement, with my obsession with not leaving the cabin.

It took for me to think of that dream, the one I swore was real where I had died. I remembered what Lev had said, and at the time, it didn't make sense.

"I can't leave," I said. "I can't walk away."

"Sometimes you must. You need to step away for the better, for the good."

Lev.

He wasn't what made me strong, he was my voice of reason. It wasn't the cabin I didn't want.

The sound of Ben dropping boxes and closing the door snapped me from my thoughts.

"Are you feeling alright? Ben asked.

"Stop that, Doctor Ben, I'm fine. I feel good."

"That's what I want to hear. This is for the best." Ben told me then handed me a box. "All right let's do this. We don't have to take everything. Just what we need and want."

"You're right."

"Nothing heavy." Ben waved a finger then grabbed his own box. "And if we need something or forget, remember, we can always come back."

I clutched that box tight to my chest and looked around, the old paint by numbers painting above the fireplace my brother Bobby had done. The rug on the floor my father purchased that my mother hated. The quilt Lev brought from his father's cabin. The drawings on the wall the kids did. My stepmother's whiskey bong which still hung on the coat rack.

So much.

It wasn't the cabin I didn't want to leave, it was everything it stood for and that was everyone I ever loved.

But walking away from the cabin wasn't walking away from them, they'd be with me.

I wasn't leaving them behind, only the cabin and it wasn't forever.

Like Ben had said, I had to remember, I could always come back.

It was my home.

Eventually…I would.

About the Author

Jacqueline Druga is a native of Pittsburgh, PA. Her works include genres of all types but she favors post-apocalypse and apocalypse writing.

For updates on new releases you can find the author on:

Facebook: @jacquelinedruga

Twitter: @gojake

www.jacquelinedruga.com